THE CASE
OF THE
GHOST GRABBERS

Also by Terrance Dicks

The Baker Street Irregulars

—— in ——

THE CASE
OF THE
GHOST GRABBERS

Terrance Dicks

ELSEVIER/NELSON BOOKS
New York

Library of Congress Cataloging in Publication Data

Dicks, Terrance.
The Baker Street Irregulars in the case of the ghost grabbers.

Originally published in 1980 under title: The case of the ghost grabbers.
Half title: The case of the ghost grabbers.
SUMMARY: When a ghost starts haunting Sir Jasper's family home, four young sleuths investigate a crime from the past and a crime they anticipate.
[1. Mystery and detective stories]   I. Title. II. Title: Case of the ghost grabbers.
PZ7.D5627Baj 1981   [Fic]   80–27224
ISBN 0–525–66729–6

Published in the United States by Elsevier-Dutton Publishing Co., Inc., 2 Park Avenue, New York, N.Y. 10016.

Printed in the U.S.A.   First U.S. edition

10 9 8 7 6 5 4 3 2 1

2142396

Contents

THE CASE
OF THE
GHOST GRABBERS

1
The Haunting

It was a wild and stormy winter's night, a night for ghosts. The man was all alone in the old dark house.

Not that he minded in the least. He was used to it. The big rambling house had been his home since childhood, and every rattle of the time-warped windowpanes, every creak of the ancient floorboards was familiar to him.

Winds howled around the house, sleet lashed against the windows, and owls hooted mournfully in the thick woods. Undisturbed by these sinister sounds, the man padded about in dressing gown and carpet slippers, checking doors and windows, making sure the burglar alarms were switched on and operating. The alarms were newly installed, and it was comforting to think that anyone trying to break in would trigger off lights and warning bells.

His tasks complete, the man walked through the long picture gallery that occupied most of the first floor. Bewhiskered Victorian worthies stared sternly at him from the walls, and here and there swords flashed, horses reared, and scarlet-coated soldiers charged heroically in some long-forgotten skirmish on the frontiers of the British Empire. There were busts and statues lining the gallery walls.

The man opened a door in the oak-paneled wall of the

gallery and passed through into the library, a book-lined room with sagging leather armchairs, an even more sagging sofa, and almost as many books on chairs and on the floor as on the shelves. The man flicked a master switch on a control panel beside the door, then went over to a corner cupboard, poured himself a large whiskey and soda and carried it, and the whiskey bottle, over to the table beside the biggest armchair. Switching on the table lamp, he sank into the chair with a weary sigh. There was a pile of papers on the table, and the man picked them up and started going through them. But the figures blurred before his eyes, and with a grimace of distaste he put the papers down and selected a dusty leather-bound volume from a pile of books. It was *A Study in Evil,* by the Reverend Henry Catchpole. On the title page was a portrait of a tall man in early-nineteenth-century dress. He studied the face, the long jaw, the jutting nose, the high temples caused by premature balding, and smiled wryly. He knew that face well. He saw it in his shaving mirror every morning.

The man in the armchair was Sir Jasper Ryde, and the man in the portrait was his great-grandfather, the first Sir Jasper, the wicked baronet.

The original Sir Jasper had drunk heavily, gambled ruinously, and seduced local maidens with monotonous regularity. He had cheated at cards, killed men in duels, and was even rumored to have dabbled in black magic. He had died spectacularly in a mysterious fire which had gutted the original family home. This house was a copy rebuilt on the same site in the mid-nineteenth century.

Sir Jasper's son had been a very different type. A

sternly upright Victorian industrialist, he had restored family fortunes in the Industrial Revolution, rebuilding the family mansion and filling it with an incredible collection of Victorian art.

And now there's me, thought the present-day Sir Jasper wryly. Thoroughly respectable, with a shy, scholarly temperament, he had inherited an impoverished estate and a family fortune almost wiped out by death duties. Like any other impoverished aristocrat he had been forced to open the family home to the public. Then there had been an astonishing stroke of luck. Hidden in the Victorian junk that filled the house was a painting by Constable. It had been discovered by chance, stolen almost immediately, recovered by some very remarkable children, and finally sold for enough to keep the old place going for a while longer.

Just my luck to be one of the respectable Rydes, thought Sir Jasper. I bet the wild ones had a lot more fun. Finding his place, he began to read. After a while his head started to nod, and eventually he dozed off, his mind whirling with confused pictures of coaches thundering through the night, sword blades flickering in the darkness, blood flowering on a white linen shirt, and piles of gold glittering evilly in the light of guttering candles.

When he awoke the room seemed very cold. He blinked and rubbed his eyes. Somehow everything seemed unreal. Serves me right for catnapping, he thought, always makes me feel awful. Cup of cocoa and bed, that's what I need.

Suddenly he heard a rumbling of wheels in the

courtyard outside the house. A late-night visitor? But there was no engine sound. Just the grinding of iron-rimmed wheels on stone flagstones . . . that and the jingle of harness, the clatter of hooves.

He was hearing a coach. A coach and horses, the kind in which the first Sir Jasper would have been driven home after a night's drinking and gambling.

He ran to the window, pulled back the faded velvet curtain and stared out. There was nothing there, of course, just the moonlit cobbled yard. On the right was the old coach house, now converted into a café for visitors . . .

Sir Jasper let go of the curtain and turned away. Overactive imagination, he thought, hearing things instead of seeing them.

There was an echoing crash from somewhere down below, as if the front door had been flung open.

Then footsteps, coming up the marble staircase, moving along the gallery toward the library door. Loud, arrogant footsteps made by booted feet.

Sir Jasper was a shy man, but he had never lacked courage. In what was perhaps the bravest act of his life, he marched to the library door and flung it open.

There was nothing to be seen but the long dark picture gallery stretching ahead. *But the footsteps were still coming toward him.* They stopped. Halfway down the gallery a shape began to form. It was a man in nineteenth-century dress, a sword in his hand. There was blood on the sword.

The man was glaring down the gallery toward the library door, his eyes glittering with a sudden chill. Sir

Jasper realized he could see *through* the figure to the oak paneling beyond.

He marched toward it.

The figure was more solid now, still glaring fixedly at him, sword in hand.

Taking a deep breath, Sir Jasper reached out to touch it. His hand went through the figure and out the other side. He snatched his hand away; the shape was still there, as solid as ever.

With a cry of alarm, Sir Jasper leaped back, heart pounding. His foot slipped and he fell, striking his head against the marble pedestal of a statue.

The last thing he saw was the glowing phantom, hovering above him.

2

On the Trail of a Ghost

"And when I woke up it had gone," concluded Sir Jasper. He looked worriedly at the four children grouped around him in the library, wondering what they made of his story.

Dan Robinson sat back in an armchair, legs crossed, chin in hands, thin face frowning in concentration. Add a deerstalker hat and a pipe, and you'd have Sherlock Holmes in the flesh.

Liz Spencer and Jeff Webster sat on each end of the sofa, like a pair of bookends. Both were fair-haired, though Jeff was broad-shouldered, stocky and solid, Liz tall and thin like Dan.

The fourth visitor was perched precariously at the top of a flight of library steps. Mickey Denning was the youngest of the group, a small, fierce, bony boy, all knees and elbows, with close-cropped wiry hair and ears like jug handles. His eyes were like saucers, and if his hair hadn't been so short it would certainly have been standing on end.

Dan, Jeff, Liz, and Mickey formed a group known as the Baker Street Irregulars. The name was taken from the group of London street Arabs who used to help Sherlock Holmes. Dan Robinson was a dedicated Sherlock Holmes fan who applied the methods of the Master to real-life crime.

The Irregulars' first success had been the recovery of the Constable painting stolen from Old Park House. Faced with a new and baffling problem, Sir Jasper had turned to his old friends for help.

It was Mickey who spoke first. "Spooks!" he breathed. "Don't know if we can do anything about spooks, can we, Dan?"

"This agency stands flat-footed upon the ground, and there it must remain," said Dan solemnly. "The world is big enough for us. No ghosts need apply."

"You mean we're not even going to try to help?" asked Liz indignantly. She looked anxiously at Sir Jasper, wondering if his feelings were hurt.

To her surprise he was smiling. "Dan was quoting from the Master. 'The Sussex Vampire,' as I recall?"

"Which turned out not to be a vampire after all," said Dan. "Maybe the same thing will happen with your ghost."

"I sincerely hope so." Sir Jasper looked around the group. "I sent down to the café for some—ah, *Coke* and *potato chips*." He pronounced the names as if they were exotic foreign delicacies. "I trust that will be acceptable?"

He produced a silver tray bearing four cans of Coke, four straws, and four bags of potato chips, and put them on the little table. "Perhaps you'd be kind enough to serve yourselves? It's a little early, but I think I'll have a whiskey and soda."

The Irregulars helped themselves. There was a brief tussle between Jeff and Mickey, who both wanted the cheese-and-onion-flavored chips—Mickey won—and they settled down to eat and drink.

Sir Jasper stood by the cupboard, staring vaguely at an empty whiskey bottle, put it down, opened a fresh one, mixed his whiskey and soda, and came back to join them.

Dan watched him worriedly. For all his cheerful manner the old boy looked pale and shaken. There were bags under his eyes, and a bruise on his forehead. "You can't have had much sleep."

"I slept surprisingly well, actually, went straight off as soon as I got into bed. I thought the whole thing was a dream when I woke up this morning. Then I felt the bump on my head."

Mickey shivered. "Don't think I could have slept, after seeing a ghost."

"Well, I must admit, I kept the light on!"

Jeff said practically, "Seems to me there are just two possibilities. Either it is a ghost or it isn't!"

Mickey finished his Coke with a satisfying gurgle. "Brilliant! A deduction worthy of old Sherlock himself."

Liz said, "If it *is* a ghost, there's nothing much we can do. But if it isn't a ghost, then someone must be faking it. All we've got to do is catch him."

Sir Jasper looked up hopefully. "A fake ghost? You mean someone's trying to frighten me? But why?"

"Maybe there's something valuable here," suggested Mickey. "They want to scare you off so they can get it."

"That's a possibility," said Jeff. "I mean you found that Constable. There could be other valuable pictures you haven't found yet."

"I'm afraid not. That thought occurred to me some time ago. I had everything in the place checked by Rundles, the art people. Oh, they made one or two finds, minor Victorian works worth a hundred or so. But definitely no masterpieces!"

"Still," persisted Jeff, "if someone *thinks* there might be something . . ."

"Then why not just come in and steal it? Why go through this charade? Besides, there's another problem. You see, after I sold the Constable, I decided to install a really efficient burglar-alarm system. No one could have got in last night without setting off the alarms." Sir Jasper nodded to the control panel by the door. There was a kind of illuminated map of the house beside it

Dan stood up. "Everything you saw and heard last night *could* have been faked. But it would take quite a lot of equipment—microphones, projectors. Did the thing leave *any* kind of physical trace?"

Sir Jasper rubbed his forehead. "Only this bruise, and of course I did that myself."

"Let's take a look at the place where it appeared."

Sir Jasper opened the library door. "I heard the coach and the footsteps when I was still in here. Then I opened the door and saw it standing in the gallery, just in front of Sir Jasper's portrait." He pointed to a bust. "That's where I fell, just by his bust."

The gallery looked empty and innocent in the morning light. Winter sunshine came through the long windows, sending bars of light across the floor. Dan walked slowly down the gallery and examined the bust. Black marble features scowled malevolently at him. He looked up at the portrait. The same features scowled down at him. Dan examined the portrait, the bust, the area around, and the whole length of the gallery from one end to the other, and then came back to the group by the library door.

They all looked expectantly at him.

"Well?" asked Sir Jasper eagerly. "Was it a real ghost or a fake?"

"Neither. It was a nightmare."

Sir Jasper's face fell. "I see." He led them back into the library.

"Look," said Dan apologetically. "I know you think you saw something—but consider the probabilities. For a start, you were feeling worried and overworked last night."

"How did you know that?"

Dan nodded toward the papers on the table. "Builders' estimates, electricians' estimates, planning permissions, some of them dated weeks ago and still not dealt with. You brought them in here last night to catch up, right?"

"I'm afraid so." Sir Jasper sighed. "You know, I never realized that having money could be just as big a problem as not having any. You know the problems I'm having with the restoration?"

Sir Jasper was using the money from the sale of the painting to restore and refurbish the enormous old house, which had been slowly falling down over the last hundred-odd years. Unfortunately the surveyor's reports had been pretty horrendous. The roof was leaking, the walls were unsafe, the foundations were soggy with rising damp, and everything in between was in disrepair as well. Sir Jasper planned to restore and refurbish the whole house, in order to attract many more visitors. In time he had hoped to make the place self-supporting, rather than a drain on his steadily diminishing capital, as it was at the moment.

The trouble was that such a colossal building job simply swallowed money, and instead of having cash to spare, Sir Jasper was beginning to feel he might have just enough—if he was lucky. In addition, the administrative side of it all was enormously complicated. Sir Jasper was a worrier by nature. Recently he was beginning to feel he was being drowned in a sea of bills, estimates, and planning permissions.

"So, there you are," Dan went on. "Tired, worried, and overworked. You start on the papers, find you just can't face it, put them aside for something more entertaining. You pick up this." Dan picked up the leather-bound volume from the table. "*A Study in Evil*—the life and times of your disreputable ancestor. You have a drink—a bigger one than you realize!" Dan tapped the empty whiskey bottle. "You were surprised to find this empty this morning." He looked around the circle of Irregulars, and then back at Sir Jasper, summing up. "Not surprisingly, you nod off—with the wicked old Sir Jasper on your mind. And you have a nightmare. The wind's howling, doors are slamming, cars going by on the road—your mind turns all this into the wicked Sir Jasper, coming home after a night on the town. You jump up, still half asleep, rush out into the gallery. There's the old boy's portrait on the wall, with his bust just in front of it. The two merge in your mind. For a minute you see Sir Jasper glaring at you. You dash forward, trip, fall onto the bust, and knock yourself out."

"I see. You think I imagined the whole thing."

Dan said carefully, "I believe you really saw and heard everything you've told us about. What I've been trying to do is explain *why* you saw and heard it."

"Congratulations, Dan. As usual, the logic of your deductions is impeccable. However, this time there is one slight flaw."

"What's that?"

"You're totally and absolutely wrong! I know what I saw and heard. I wasn't dreaming, I wasn't having hallucinations. I was wide awake."

Dan took a deep breath. "All right. Let's accept that, for the moment. As Jeff said, we're left with two possibilities. Either there is a real ghost—or someone's faking it. We can't do much about the first one—real ghosts aren't in my line, particularly as I don't believe in them anyway. So we're left with the second choice—it's all a fake."

"I thought we'd established there couldn't be any fakery," objected Jeff. "Because of all the burglar alarms."

"That's right. But it's still the only possibility we're left with—and it happens to be the only one we can investigate anyway."

"How?" asked Liz. "How do we investigate a ghost—real *or* fake?"

"All the ghosts I've heard of aren't satisfied with just a single performance. They keep coming back for an encore."

Mickey gave him a look of alarm. "Are you thinking what I'm thinking you're thinking?"

"That's right. We're all going to spend a night in a

haunted house. Provided Sir Jasper will have us, of course."

"I'd be delighted," said Sir Jasper promptly. "We shall lie in wait for the phantom together."

The rest of the Irregulars weren't delighted at all, and there was an immediate outburst of protest. It would all be a waste of time; their parents wouldn't allow it. Not that anyone was scared, of course.

Ruthlessly, Dan overrode their objections. "All you've got to do is tell your parents that we've all been invited to stay at Old Park House. We'll all be together, and they know Sir Jasper's a friend of ours. There's no need for you to mention ghosts at all."

Jeff, Liz, and Mickey looked resignedly at each other. Dan was right. Not that their parents were snobs, of course. . . . But Sir Jasper was still very much the local squire, and no one would object very hard to their paying a visit to the aristocracy. All three had more or less simultaneous visions of their parents' casually mentioning the visit to their friends.

Dan smiled at the solemn faces. Seldom had the Irregulars started a case with less enthusiasm. Dan himself had no worries at all. As convinced a rationalist as his idol Sherlock Holmes, he could see only two possible results to this investigation. The first, and most likely, was that they'd find nothing at all. The second was that someone was trying to scare Sir Jasper with fake ghosts—and that could be very interesting indeed.

Sir Jasper was just offering to phone their parents personally when there was a deferential cough from the door. A stocky, gray-haired man was standing in the doorway. He had blunt, open features, square, work-hardened hands, and he wore a shiny blue suit with a slide rule projecting from the top pocket. "Excuse me, Sir Jasper, but we were going to go through those estimates. . . ."

Sir Jasper ran a hand over his bald head. "Good grief, so we were. I didn't finish working on them, I'm afraid, but we can make a start." He looked helplessly at Dan. "If you'll excuse me? Provided your parents agree, I'll expect you all back here this evening."

As they went down the gallery they could hear Sir Jasper saying, "The thing is, Mr. Chipsted, I don't see why you have to spend so much time on the foundations. I should have thought the roof was the first priority."

Chipsted's voice had all the weary patience of the professional trying to explain to the ignorant layman. "Naturally the roof's important, and it'll be seen to all in good time. But what's the use of keeping the rain out of the top if the damp's seeping up the walls from the foundations? It's damp that does your *lasting* damage."

They went down the stairs.

Outside in the frosty sunshine, they crunched their way down the gravel drive that led away from the house. "Poor old Sir Jasper," said Liz. "What with spooks and builders, he's really getting clobbered."

Dan nodded absently. He was examining the gravel for traces of carriage wheels. There was nothing to be seen. Still, maybe a ghostly coach wouldn't leave solid tracks.

Mickey was jumping up and down shivering. Despite the cold, he wore only his usual jeans and sweater, and he was so thin that his bones were rattling with the cold.

"Talk about shuddering skeletons," said Jeff. "You'll scare the ghost more than it'll scare you!"

"Do you really think we'll see anything, Dan?" asked Liz.

"Who knows? At the witching hour, when graveyards yawn and give up their dead . . ."

"Shut up," said Jeff uneasily.

Dan smiled. Strange that the stolid Jeff should be so susceptible.

Dan didn't know it yet, but his own skepticism was to be considerably shaken by the events of the coming night.

3
A Night in a Haunted House

Three subdued children and a big black, shapeless dog made their way up the road through the woods toward Old Park House. It was already dark, and rustling trees and hooting owls made the journey a sinister one.

Dan was glad he'd decided to bring his dog Baskerville, and gladder still that he'd met Liz and Jeff at the entrance to the lane. It's one thing to be skeptical about ghosts in broad daylight. But after dark, things feel very different. It was an uneasy party that assembled in the hall of Old Park House.

It had been easy enough getting permission for the outing. For one thing, the Irregulars often spent nights at each other's houses, especially at holiday time, and their parents were used to their being away. And as Dan had predicted, Sir Jasper's name had worked wonders. Sir Jasper had telephoned all the parents personally, winning them over with his courtly old-fashioned charm, and managing to make the whole thing sound like a royal garden party—an invitation you couldn't possibly refuse.

Mickey's mum had been a bit sticky at first. Mickey came from a large old-fashioned Cockney family, and his mother was convinced that the only safe place for her numerous brood at night was tucked up in their own beds, with her keeping a watchful eye on them. Even

16

Mickey's eldest brother had some job if he wanted to spend a night away from home, and he was twenty-five.

However, Sir Jasper had won her over, and at last she'd agreed that Mickey could go. But she'd had her revenge. When Mickey arrived, the others hardly recognized him. He had been scrubbed until he positively gleamed, and he was wearing a blue serge suit so new that it squeaked, black shiny shoes, and a shirt and tie.

Mickey glared defiantly around the circle of astonished faces. "All right, all right, I can see what you're thinking. But no cracks, okay? Otherwise there'll be some brand-new ghosts haunting this place!"

Dan's mouth twitched, and Jeff made a mighty effort to keep his face straight. But neither of them spoke. They knew a desperate man when they saw one.

"I think you look very smart," said Liz loyally. She felt a certain sympathy for Mickey. After a brief battle of wills with her mother, she had reluctantly changed into her best dark-blue dress and brushed her hair. Liz's mother, a crusading freelance journalist, had explained that although she personally wasn't in the least impressed by outdated aristocracy, there were certain standards of behavior . . .

Liz pointed to the school satchel on Mickey's shoulder. "What have you got in there?"

"Oh, just things . . ." said Mickey vaguely.

Jeff reached out and twitched it from his shoulder. "Come on, let's have a look."

He emptied the satchel onto the ticket counter. Out fell a packet of salt, a drum of pepper, a hymnbook, a Mickey Mouse flashlight, a packet of peppermints, and a number of little wooden sticks. "What's all this then?"

Mickey grabbed the satchel and began stuffing things back inside. "Had to improvise, didn't I? My mum doesn't use garlic, so I brought salt and pepper instead. I thought the hymnbook would do for a Bible."

"All very enterprising," said Dan. "All I brought was a nice big flashlight!"

Jeff picked up one of the little sticks and examined it. "It's a lolly-stick! A sharpened lolly-stick!"

"Well, you have to have a sharp stake," said Mickey scathingly. "Don't you know anything?"

"Garlic and stakes are for vampires, you idiot, not common or garden spooks. Anyway, a sharp lolly-stick wouldn't do you much good—not unless they were mini vampires!"

"I tried to get hold of a broom handle, but Mum wouldn't part with it. I had to sacrifice some of my collection."

"Collection? What do you collect those things for?"

"Playing lolly-sticks, of course. Here, grab hold of that. Hold it out in front of you. No, two hands, you twit, hold it at each end."

Jeff held out his lollipop stick, and Mickey gripped another one in the same way. Then he brought it crashing down like a mini quarterstaff, splintering the one in Jeff's hands.

Jeff looked down at the broken stick. "Is that it?"

"Well, of course that's it. I won! Very skillful game, lolly-sticks, I happen to be school champion!"

"Skilled!" scoffed Jeff. "Here, let me try. You hold the stick this time." Jeff tried to repeat Mickey's feat, but to his indignant astonishment, it was his stick and not Mickey's that broke.

"See?" said Mickey. "Not so easy as it looks, is it?"

Dan picked up a lollipop stick and studied it thoughtfully. "If you hit with the sharp edge, you concentrate the force. Let's have a go!"

They had another round of lollipop sticks, with Mickey explaining the finer points of the game.

Liz watched with lofty scorn. "I don't know how you can all be so childish . . ."

Suddenly they heard footsteps and voices from above. Hastily they shoved the lollipop sticks back into Mickey's satchel and looked up.

Sir Jasper was coming down the stairs, talking to a tall, smartly dressed man wearing a green porkpie hat and carrying a briefcase under his arm. "I'm sorry to keep you all waiting. This is Mr. Shepherd; his firm installed the alarm system. Mr. Shepherd, Elizabeth Spencer, Daniel Robinson, Jeffrey Webster, and Michael Denning —and, of course, Baskerville."

Baskerville gave a *woof* that echoed around the building.

Mr. Shepherd acknowledged the introductions with an absent nod, and turned back to Sir Jasper.

"Look, Squire, I don't know what's got you worried, but I hope I've been able to put your mind at rest."

"I called Mr. Shepherd earlier," explained Sir Jasper. "He was good enough to come out here and check over the new alarm system for me. He says everything's functioning perfectly."

" 'Course it is," said Shepherd impatiently. "Just been installed, brand-new system tailor-made to the client's requirements, up-to-date equipment. You know our motto, Squire. 'Let Shepherds watch by night'!"

"How does the system work?" asked Dan.

"It's a new sonic system, sonny, very complicated; you wouldn't understand."

"Try me."

Shepherd looked hard at him. Sir Jasper said gently, "If you wouldn't mind, Mr. Shepherd. Dan's a particular friend of mine."

Shepherd sighed. "Anything for a customer." He fished a brochure from his briefcase and spread it out on the counter. "It's all controlled from the master panel, you see, which in this case is installed in the library. Now, every door and window is linked into the main circuit here by an ultrasonic circuit." Mr. Shepherd went on for some time, losing himself, perhaps deliberately, in a maze of technicalities. But when he finished speaking, the main message was clear enough. Every door and every window, every possible means of entry into Old Park Hall, from the basement to the roof, was covered by the sonic alarm system.

"Could anyone interfere with the system?" asked Jeff. "Cut a wire or something?"

"Haven't you been listening? No exterior wires to cut, that's the beauty of it. The only way anyone could interfere would be by getting at the main power installation down in the basement or the control panel in the library, and they're both protected by the system itself. Believe me, once Sir Jasper's switched on, a mouse couldn't get in without setting off the alarm." He looked hard at Dan. "Satisfied, sonny?"

"Not quite," said Dan. "Suppose we test it?"

For a moment it looked as if Mr. Shepherd were going to explode. "Test it?" he roared. "Test it?" He caught Sir Jasper's eye and mastered himself with a mighty effort. "All right, sonny, if you want to test it, we'll test it. Outside, the lot of you. Give me a couple of minutes to lock up and set the alarms, then try to get in anywhere and anyway you like. If you can open a door or a window so much as a crack without triggering the system, I'll . . . I'll . . ."

"Eat your hat?" suggested Mickey helpfully. "I mean, they call them porkpies, don't they?"

Shepherd gave him a withering glare and pointed to the door.

"Come on," said Dan. "Perhaps you'd better keep Baskerville here, Sir Jasper. Stay, Baskerville."

Baskerville gave a disappointed whine, but sat obediently where he was. Dan let the others out the front door and down the steps, and onto the graveled drive that led up to the big old house.

With a cheery wave, Sir Jasper closed the front door behind them, and seconds later they heard the rattle of the locks.

The Irregulars stood huddled in a little group in the pool of light caused by the carriage lamps beside the door. The dark woods seemed to gather threateningly around the house. It was very cold, and their breath rose like steam in the gaslight.

Dan looked at his watch. "No point in trying the main door, that's bound to be covered. Let's work our way around the back. By the time we get there they should have the alarm set. Let's see if this sonic alarm system's all it's cracked up to be."

4
The Test

Old Park House had one long central wing, with two smaller wings set at right angles to the main block, one at each end. Facing the house, you were looking at the main hall, with the public rooms on either side. A curved marble staircase led up to the first-floor gallery and Sir Jasper's library and study. The wing on your left held living quarters, the one on the right was the old coach house, now converted into a café. The wicked Sir Jasper's carriage still stood in the center of the big stone-flagged room, incongruous amid the plastic-topped tables.

Seen from the back, the three wings of the house formed three sides of a square, or rather an oblong, enclosing a cobbled yard. The missing long side of the oblong was filled in by a row of miscellaneous buildings, sheds, and outhouses, detached from the main body of the house, including the garage for Sir Jasper's ancient and seldom-used Rolls and the battered Volkswagen Beetle he usually drove.

The back of the house was even more gloomy than the front, lighted only by the pale gleam of a restored gas lamp.

Dan glanced at his watch again and looked around. "Okay, they've had enough time. Where do we start?"

They all looked at each other, not sure what to do next. Jeff grinned. "I suppose we're all so geared up to catching crooks, it's hard to start thinking like a burglar."

As might have been expected, it was Mickey who adapted most quickly to a life of crime. He fished an enormous jackknife from his pocket and opened it. "That little window up there, just over the café. I'll try that." Clasping the knife in his teeth like a miniature pirate, Mickey shinned nimbly up a drainpipe and put one knee on the sill of a tiny first-floor window. Clinging to the pipe with one hand, he took the knife from his teeth and tried to lever back the window catch.

Immediately lights came on in the little room, and there was the clangor of an alarm from inside the house. Mickey was so surprised he nearly fell off the drainpipe. As it was, he dropped the open jackknife with a clatter, making everyone jump back.

Sliding down the pipe, Mickey recovered his knife and looked at the others. "Well, they've covered that one all right; I barely touched that window. Someone else have a go."

The light in the little room went out and the alarm stopped ringing. The black bulk of the big old house loomed smugly above them, as if daring them to have another try. They tried.

Jeff crossed the yard and tried to force a side door of the living quarters.

Liz tried a ground-floor café window.

Dan, in an attempt to be really cunning, went down some steps to a sort of basement yard and tried to lift the cover of a hatch leading to the cellars.

In each case there was the same result. Lights came on and an alarm sounded inside the house. They made several other tries, all with the same result, and eventually had to give up.

They trooped around to the front of the house and found the front door open again. Shepherd stood beside Sir Jasper in the hall, an expression of smug triumph on his face. "See?" he said simply. "Window of the staff toilet in the café, side entrance to the residential wing, ground-floor window in the café, disused coal hatch." He reeled off all the places where they'd tried to break in.

Jeff stared at him. "How did you know all that?"

"Come and see." Shepherd led them upstairs, through the darkened gallery and into the library. Inside the door, just to the left, was the small control panel with, beside it, the illuminated plan of the house. "All shows up on here, see? Any interference with the sonic circuits, and a light flashes on the display chart, shows you exactly where they're trying it on."

Dan shook his head in admiration. "All right, Mr. Shepherd, you win. If I ever win the lottery, I'll hire your firm to guard all my treasures."

Mr. Shepherd glowed visibly at the compliment. "Tell you the truth, the system's *too* sensitive, if anything. Could be triggered by a bird flying into a window, or the wind rattling a door. Still, better the odd false alarm than no alarm when you need it, eh? Well, if everybody's happy, I'll be on my way."

Sir Jasper thanked Mr. Shepherd profusely and showed him out, locking the main door behind him. He came back up the stairs and into the library and threw the master switch on the alarm. "There you are, Dan. I hope you're convinced that if we do see or hear anything tonight, it won't be caused by some local delinquents trooping around in white sheets."

"I believe you, it's quite a system. Excuse my asking, but why invest in anything so elaborate? I mean, since you've established that there isn't anything really valuable in the house . . ."

"Ah, but people might *think* there was, you see. They might assume that where one valuable painting was found, there could be more. I don't want a procession of the criminal fraternity trooping around here every night, trying their luck. If you remember, I got a very nasty crack on the skull when we last had a robbery." Sir Jasper rubbed a tiny scar on the crown of his bald head. "Besides, it wasn't as expensive as you might think. I got several estimates, and the Shepherd system was the cheapest, as well as the most up-to-date. Mr. Shepherd said he'd never had the chance to install his new system in such a big house before, and the job would bring his firm some prestige. He offered me very good terms. . . ." Sir Jasper looked at his watch. "Still some time till the witching hour, I see. How about a little refreshment? I persuaded my housekeeper to leave us a cold collation."

"A cold what?" whispered Mickey uneasily, fearing some exotic foreign dish. But he needn't have worried. The ingredients of Sir Jasper's cold collation were familiar enough. Beef sandwiches, slices of cold veal and ham pie, and sausage rolls. There was even a big thermos flask of cocoa. "I thought it would be more acceptable on a winter's night than Coke," said Sir Jasper. He glanced at them anxiously, as if wondering whether he'd committed some social error. He'd had little to do with children before making the acquaintance of the Irregulars, and tended to treat them like a party of Balinese diplomats, with strange dietary customs of their own.

"That's perfectly all right," said Dan solemnly. "We don't actually *live* on Coke and potato chips—though I suppose some people would if they had the chance."

He glanced at Mickey, who shot him a reproachful glare, but said nothing—he couldn't speak because his mouth was already full of pie.

Soon everyone was eating and drinking steadily. There was something very comforting about solid food and hot cocoa on a winter's night, thought Liz— especially when you were bracing yourself for an encounter with the supernatural. "What are we actually going to do?" she asked. "I've never been on a ghost hunt before."

"Maybe we should split up," suggested Jeff. "Post ourselves in different parts of the building. I mean, in a place this size, a dozen ghosts could be haunting away like mad with no one to see them."

Dan put down his cocoa. "I think we should all stay right here. For one thing, if we split up and hang around in dark corners by ourselves, we'll see ghosts for sure. In a place like this anyone would."

"Too true," said Liz. "I saw at least six coming up the drive!"

"Besides, as far as I can make out, any ghost worth its

salt *wants* to be seen. I mean what's the point in haunting away without an audience? No, we'll all sit tight, right here. We don't have to rush around looking for ghosts. If there is one here, it will come and find us!"

There was an uneasy silence. Still, it was hard to feel spooky for long in the warm, brightly lighted study with the coal fire blazing.

It was past eleven by the time supper was over. They stacked the used crockery on the tray and put it back on the serving trolley. For a time they sat around chatting, but after a while conversation flagged, as much from drowsiness as anything else. It was late, they were warm and cozy and full of good food, and soon heads began to nod.

Sir Jasper sat dozing in his armchair, much as he had done the night before, book on his lap and spectacles slipping from his nose.

Liz and Jeff sprawled on opposite ends of the sofa. It was overstuffed and bulging, and the worn velvet was very soft. You could sink into it, like into a feather mattress. Soon they too were asleep.

Mickey was also fast asleep, curled up on the rug in front of the fire with Baskerville, arms clasping the big dog like some enormous furry bolster. Even Baskerville slept, his head resting between his paws.

Only Dan stayed wide awake. He sat in the smaller of the two armchairs, legs crossed, chin cupped in one hand, quite motionless except for his eyes. He looked at his sleeping companions, at the flickering glow of the dying fire, at the display chart of the alarm system, at the closed study door and the curtained window.

Most of all he looked at the old-fashioned clock on the

mantelpiece. Its tick was very loud in the silent room. He checked the clock against his watch. Just one minute to midnight.

The old clock whirred and clicked and began to chime. One . . . two . . . three . . . The sleepers stirred uneasily, but none of them awoke. Nine . . . ten . . . eleven . . . After the twelfth stroke died away there was a moment of total silence, as if time were suspended.

Then the lights in the room began to dim. The room grew darker and darker until it was lighted only by the glowing coals of the fire.

Suddenly iron-rimmed wheels rumbled on the cobbles outside. There was the clatter of horses' hooves, the jingle of harness. . . .

Baskerville raised his head and gave a low, blood-curdling growl.

5
The Ghost Walks Again

Dan jumped to his feet, snatching up his light. Although events seemed to be repeating themselves, he didn't propose to follow Sir Jasper's timetable. If the ghost was going to appear, he wanted to be there when it happened. "Come on, Baskerville."

The dog flattened his head between his paws.

"Baskerville!" called Dan sharply. Although he didn't believe in ghosts, it would be a comfort to have the big dog at his side.

Baskerville gave a low whine and refused to move. The sound of heavy, booted footsteps came from outside the door.

Opening the library door was one of the hardest things he had ever done in his life, but somehow Dan managed it. He stared into the darkness of the gallery, and as his eyes adjusted to the gloom he began to pick out the rows of portraits and battle scenes, the statues and busts ranged along the wall.

He could still hear the footsteps. They seemed to be moving *away* from him, as if the invisible phantom had come up to the library door and then turned back. Suddenly a glow appeared at the far end of the gallery. It brightened and solidified into a definite form, a human figure. It was a man in old-fashioned clothes, some kind of riding coat, riding breeches, and high boots. The thin face with its beaky nose was dead white, and the black eyes seemed to glitter madly.

In its hand was a drawn sword.

Dan stood transfixed in the doorway, the flashlight gripped tightly in his hand. The flashlight! He switched it on, and a beam of light shot along the gallery, illuminating the figure. It didn't vanish under the light. It simply stood there motionless in the light beam. It was completely solid, real, three-dimensional—yet Dan realized that he could see through the figure to the oak paneling on the wall behind it.

Suddenly the figure vanished.

Dan ran down the gallery toward it and shone his light all around the area where the phantom had appeared. But the figure had gone, leaving no traces behind it. Maybe traces were too much to hope for, he thought. After all, would you get ghostly mud on the boots of a ghost?

Then he heard the footsteps again. They seemed to be climbing the marble staircase outside the gallery door. Dan rushed out onto the landing. In front of him the staircase curved downward to the public rooms and entrance hall, upward to the third story.

The ghost stood at the top of the staircase, looking down at him. It was in exactly the same pose as in the gallery, the drawn sword in its hand. It vanished again. Dan could hear footsteps moving upward out of sight.

Drawing a deep breath, he began climbing the staircase. The top floor of Old Park House was largely disused. In the good old days it had been domestic quarters, rows of cramped attic bedrooms for the legions of servants who had toiled to keep the aristocracy comfortable. Upstairs maids, downstairs maids, in-between maids, footmen, pantry boys . . . this is where they'd snatched a few hours of sleep, between a late finish and an early start.

Now these upper rooms were mostly used for storage, providing a home for the pile of junk too scruffy to be put on display. Sir Jasper's grandfather had been a Victorian millionaire with a strong collector's instinct and a good deal more money than sense. The present-day Sir Jasper had put anything remotely valuable or interesting on show, but there were still piles of things that were not really worth displaying but too good to throw away.

Dan found himself moving along a central corridor lined with doors, some closed and some open. He flashed his light beam into the rooms, lighting up tottering piles of furniture—chairs, tables, chests of drawers, cabinets and cupboards and display cases, stuffed animals and mounted fishes, their glass eyes glinting sinisterly in the light.

He paused, irresolute—and the ghost appeared again. It was standing by an open doorway at the end of the corridor, still staring fixedly at him.

Then it disappeared.

Cautiously Dan moved down the corridor, shining the light ahead of him. He had a feeling that he was being led somewhere—or perhaps "lured" would be a better word. But why? Only one way to find out.

Dan walked steadily to the room at the end of the corridor and went inside. It was a larger room than most of the others, and had been crammed full with assorted junk. Dan stood in a kind of central canyon, with piles of ancient furniture all around him, most of it broken in some way. Tables with missing legs, cupboards with no fronts, armless armchairs . . .

He stood flashing the light around him. There was no sign of the ghost, no sound of footsteps. . . .

Suddenly the door slammed closed behind him. Something smashed the flashlight from his hand and it fell and broke, leaving him in total darkness. A peal of maniacal laughter filled the room. The mad laughter merged with a rumbling sound, and suddenly Dan realized—the mountain of furniture was on the move.

Frantically he flung himself toward the door, groped for the handle and flung it open—just as a cascade of furniture tumbled down upon him.

Dan stumbled and fell, trapped by some heavy weight across his legs. Something struck the back of his head and he fell into blackness.

Baskerville threw back his head and gave a long, shuddering howl.

Sir Jasper, Liz, Jeff, and Mickey jerked awake to find the door standing open and Dan nowhere to be seen.

Sir Jasper ran out into the gallery, the others close behind him. He flicked a row of switches by the door and the gallery became ablaze with light. There was no sign of Dan. Baskerville began barking loudly. "Find him, boy!" said Jeff.

Barking furiously, the big dog led them down the gallery, out of the room, and up the stairs.

Sir Jasper switched on more lights. At the end of the corridor they saw Dan lying in the middle of a litter of furniture. Baskerville was standing over him, licking his face. Dan's face was white and still, his eyes were closed, his forehead smeared with blood.

Dan Robinson floated back up to consciousness, aware only that his head and ankle ached, and that he was in bed. Not his usual bed either. Normally Dan slept in a quilted sleeping bag—he looked after his own room, and it simplified bedmaking. But this bed had sheets, clean, white and starched, and he was tucked in so tightly he could hardly move.

He opened his eyes and saw a dark-complexioned woman in a nylon uniform industriously polishing his bedside table. Dan tried to say "Hello," but it came out as a sort of croak. The woman gave him a dazzling smile, said something he didn't understand, and went off. A few minutes later a nurse bustled in, took his temperature, felt his pulse, gave him a drink of water and a large glass bottle, waited till he'd finished with both, and bustled out of the room.

Dan was just beginning to doze off when she reappeared, this time with a large young man in a white coat. He shone a light in Dan's eye, felt his pulse, and said briskly, "All right, Sonny-Jim. What's your name?"

"Well, it's not Sonny-Jim, for a start," said Dan crossly.

"Come on," coaxed the man. "What's your name? Can you remember your address? What happened to you?"

Dan stared blankly at him, wondering what was going on. Didn't they keep proper records in this place? Had he been found wandering in the street, or dumped on the steps by a passing car?

"Don't worry," said the young doctor soothingly. "Things'll soon start coming back."

Suddenly Dan realized—he'd had a knock on the head, been unconscious for a while, and they were wondering if he'd lost his memory. For a moment Dan was tempted to stare vacantly into space and mutter, "Who am I?" in the best Hollywood style, but he decided it would cause too many complications.

In a brisk voice he rattled off his name, address, and telephone number, throwing in his weight, height, and collar size for good measure. "As for what happened, I was exploring a disused room in Old Park House when a pile of furniture fell on me."

The doctor grinned. "You realize you're breaking all the rules? You're supposed to lie there all dopy and mutter, 'Where am I?' "

Dan looked around. "Well, I'm obviously in a hospital, and since I'm in a private room and my parents think private medicine is immoral, I imagine it was fixed up by Sir Jasper Ryde. I can smell hospital food and hear trollies, so it's lunchtime, and I've been out for about twelve hours. Now, what's wrong with my ankle, and when can I go home?"

"Nothing much wrong with your brain box, is there?" said the young doctor admiringly. "Well, all your deductions are correct, Young Sherlock. Your ankle's badly swollen, may be just bruised, but there could be a hairline fracture; we won't know till we do the X rays. You had a nasty knock on the head and you were out cold for a long time, so we're keeping you in here for a couple of days for observation, in case there's any delayed-action effect. All right?"

Before Dan could protest that it wasn't all right, the doctor got up. "You've got six visitors waiting to see you, and I'll allow half an hour's visiting time. How do you want them, all in a lump or five minutes each?"

"How about ten minutes parents, ten minutes Sir Jasper, and ten minutes kids?"

"Right!" The doctor went out. Dan's parents came in, and he spent the next five minutes reassuring them that he wasn't at death's door. Apparently Sir Jasper was in a state of agonized guilt, had insisted on a private room and the best of treatment, and hadn't stopped apologizing to them since the accident had happened.

"Silly old twit," said Dan affectionately. "Wasn't his fault anyway. Anyway, I'm all right, really, just a few bumps and bruises."

"How did it happen?" asked Dan's father. "What were you doing, playing hide and seek?"

"Something like that," said Dan vaguely. Obviously no one had mentioned ghosts to them, and it seemed a good idea to keep it that way.

Dan's mother looked around the room. "He insisted on you having this private room, heaven knows how much it's costing him, and it's ridiculous really, since one gets exactly the same treatment . . ."

After more reassurances from Dan, his parents took themselves off, leaving behind a basket of fruit and a bunch of grapes and promising to come back later that evening.

As soon as they were gone, Sir Jasper rushed in. "My dear Dan! What can I possibly say! That I should have been responsible for involving you in such danger! How are your injuries? Have you seen a doctor? Is there anything I can get for you? Fruit, books, a television set?"

"Look, I'm fine," said Dan awkwardly. "It wasn't your fault. It was my idea to go ghost hunting, and I shouldn't have gone rushing off on my own like that anyway."

It took Dan quite some time to calm the old boy down.

Sir Jasper lowered his voice. "What *happened,* Dan?"

Dan told him, and when he'd finished Sir Jasper said, "You saw it then? You saw the ghost?"

"I saw the figure of a man in old-fashioned clothes. I heard the sound of a carriage outside, I heard footsteps, and right at the end I heard laughter. I'm not yet convinced all that adds up to a ghost."

"Perhaps I should leave Old Park," said Sir Jasper worriedly. "Close the place down and move out."

"No! That's the last thing you should do. Just carry on as normal until we find out what's going on."

"But you're immobilized now . . ."

"Not for long. Anyway, there are the others, aren't there? What about Jeff and Liz and Mickey?"

"All waiting outside and eager to see you." After renewed apologies and offers to send in every imaginable comfort, Sir Jasper left. Before he went, Dan extracted a reluctant promise that he'd carry on exactly as normal, keeping the house open to the public and continuing to live there, until Dan had a chance to investigate further. He also promised to send over *A Study in Evil,* so that Dan could learn more about the man whose ghost was supposed to have clobbered him.

No sooner was he gone than Jeff, Liz, and Mickey rushed into the room. For some reason, Mickey carried a large plastic bag. Liz had a pile of thrillers. Liz and Jeff were both worried by Dan's white face and bandaged head, and he had to spend a few minutes reassuring *them.*

Mickey, however, had no time for frills. Pausing only to grab some grapes, he said, "Come on, Robbo, what happened? Did the ghost clobber you?"

For the second time Dan recounted what had happened to him.

When he'd finished, Liz reacted just like Sir Jasper. "So you actually *saw* the ghost!"

"I heard sounds and saw an image. Nothing that couldn't have been produced by natural means."

"What, even the ghost itself? You said it was a three-dimensional figure—you could see around it as well as through it."

"It could very well have been a holograph projection. You remember, we went to that exhibition last term?"

"That's right," said Mickey. "They had this vase on a stand. Looked absolutely solid, but you could put your hand right through it."

"And I suppose the carriage and the footsteps and the laughter could have been recordings," said Liz slowly. "Like in *Son et Lumière.*"

"That's right."

"I think you're forgetting something," said Jeff. "Look, Dan, I'm as skeptical about ghosts as you are, and of course everything you saw *could* have been faked. But we were all locked up inside a completely burglar-proofed house. If someone was faking ghosts—how did they get in?"

6

The Powers of Evil

Dan was silent for a moment. Then he said obstinately, "I don't know—yet. But they must have—because they did! Maybe the alarms broke down or something."

It sounded feeble as soon as he said it, and Dan wasn't surprised when Jeff shook his head. "We'd just checked, remember. And Sir Jasper rechecked afterward."

"Well, maybe they were there all along."

Jeff shook his head again. "The workmen would have seen anyone in the cellars, and Mr. Shepherd went over the whole house when he was checking the alarms."

"All right," said Dan wearily. "Tell me what happened to you."

"I'll tell you," said Mickey importantly. "Old Baskerville started howling his head off, and we all woke up to find you gone. We came out to look for you, followed Baskerville upstairs, and found you flat out in the middle of a pile of old junk."

Liz took up the story. "Sir Jasper rushed back down to the library and dialed nine-nine-nine. The rest of us had a quick look around, but we didn't see or hear anything." It had been a very quick look around, actually, Liz remembered. No one had much desire to go prowling around those dark and sinister rooms, crowded with oddly shaped pieces of furniture. Not after finding Dan laid out like a corpse.

"Then we went back to the library," said Jeff. "While we were waiting for the ambulance, I got Sir Jasper to check the alarms. According to the control panel they were in full working order."

"They were working all right," said Mickey. "Don't you remember, the ambulance men set 'em all off when they hammered on the door? There was a heck of a racket."

"The thing is, Dan," said Jeff, "if it was all a fake, they'd need special equipment—lights, projectors, microphones, stuff like that. How did they get it all in and out again without setting off the alarm?"

"Maybe they left it hidden somewhere in the house."

"Sir Jasper got the workmen to search the house this morning. They didn't find a thing."

Mickey looked solemnly at Dan. "Face it, Robbo, you got clobbered by a genuine ghost."

Dan looked exasperatedly at the solemn faces of his three friends. "You act like some old spinsters at a séance. Couple of bumps in the night, and you're all ready to believe in ghosts. Well, I'm the one who actually *saw* the thing, and I'm going to take a lot more convincing."

Jeff sighed. "All right, Sherlock, what's your theory?"

"Someone wants Sir Jasper out of Old Park House," said Dan simply.

Mickey's eyes widened. "You mean there's another masterpiece among all that junk after all?"

"I doubt it. Sir Jasper had it all examined, remember? But there's something valuable there all the same."

Mickey was jumping up and down in excitement. "The wicked old Sir Jasper's buried treasure! Boxes crammed full with gold and jewels." He began hopping around the room on one leg, cackling, "Pieces of eight, me hearties, pieces of eight!" He'd seen *Treasure Island* on television.

Jeff grabbed him and plunked him back in a chair. "Sit down and shut up, Mickey. The old villain wasn't a pirate—and this isn't a film." He turned to Dan. "What do you think this mysterious treasure is, then?"

"I've no idea what it is, Jeff, not yet. But I'm going to find out—and I'm going to find out who's after it."

"How? I gather they're going to keep you in here for a day or two."

"I shall just have to be Mycroft instead of Sherlock, won't I?"

"Who?" said Mickey blankly.

"Mycroft was Sherlock's older brother. He could have been an even greater detective, but he never went out because he was too lazy to leave his club."

"Or Nero Wolfe," said Jeff, who occasionally read a detective story or two himself. "He was too fat to go out. He had this brave, handsome, tough assistant called Archie Goodwin to do all the hard work." It was obvious whom Jeff saw in this role.

"Well, I suppose Hercule Poirot never rushed about all that much," said Liz. "You can just lie here and do it all with ze little gray cells. By the way, I've brought you a few Agatha Christies, Dan. Conan Doyle's not the only one worth reading."

Dan looked around the little group. "I've still got my faithful Irregulars, haven't I—unless you're all going to give up detective work for crystal gazing."

"All right, Dan, knock it off," said Jeff. "What do you want us to do?"

"Stay close to Sir Jasper, for a start. Convince your parents my accident was just an accident—we were playing hide and seek and some old furniture fell on me. For Pete's sake, no one mention ghosts. Get them to let you stay at Old Park tonight, as well. Say Sir Jasper wants you to stay the weekend."

Liz drew a deep breath. One night in a haunted house was bad enough—but two? Still, they couldn't let Dan down. "All right. Then what?"

"Well, don't do what I did, for a start, and go rushing off by yourselves. Stick together, whatever happens, especially at night. Just keep your eye out for anyone and anything suspicious."

Mickey finished the last of the grapes and stood up. "Don't you worry, Robbo, we'll look after things. By the time you get out of here, we'll have it all solved." He took the plastic bag from under his seat. "I've brought you a souvenir. Sir Jasper said it was okay." From the bag Mickey produced a shallow bowl with big curved handles on each side. It was made of the kind of earthenware china that seems almost as heavy as stone, and it was embossed with an ornate crest, presumably the arms of the Ryde family. "It was just beside your head when we found you knocked out," explained Mickey. "I reckon it was what actually clunked you. Must have been balanced on top of the pile."

Dan grinned. "Well, it's very kind of you, Mickey, but I'm sure the hospital facilities are quite adequate."

"What are you talking about? I thought it would make a nice flower vase."

"Maybe it would, but that's not what it was designed for. It's supposed to go under the bed, not beside it."

"What for?"

Briefly Dan explained the mysteries of sanitation before the invention of flush toilets.

Mickey was fascinated. "How did they, well, you know—get rid of it, after?"

"Well, in really early times they just yelled 'Gardey-loo!' and chucked the contents out of the nearest window. That's where the word 'loo' comes from, you know."

"Crikey," said Mickey. "You'd have to watch out on a stroll through old London town!"

"They're quite valuable, now," said Liz. "A lot of people collect them."

Jeff put the chamber pot on Dan's windowsill. "There you are. It'll add a touch of class. The nurse can put your flowers in it!"

At this point the nurse appeared and chased the visitors away, since they'd already had a lot more time than their ten minutes.

The Irregulars left, promising to call and report next day, and Dan sank back on his pillow. His head was throbbing, and he was more tired than he had realized.

As he sank back into sleep, his mind began replaying the events of the previous night. He heard the ghostly footsteps, saw again the glowing figure with its hate-filled face and bloody sword. It must have been a fake . . . it *must!* But how?

Liz looked at the old carriage and shivered. It loomed dark and sinister in the center of the empty café. It was easy to imagine it rattling over the cobbles on some dark and stormy night, with the evil Sir Jasper lurking inside.

Untroubled by any such imaginings, Jeff and Mickey were tucking into ham pie and potato chips. So far they'd just followed Dan's instructions, persuaded their families the weekend was still on, and made their way back to Old Park House. By the time they'd actually got there it was well past lunchtime, and Sir Jasper was busily engaged with Mr. Chipsted and a gang of rather villainous-looking workmen, who seemed bent on knocking the old house down rather than repairing it. Reluctant to disturb him, the Irregulars had stolen away and clubbed together to buy themselves lunch in the café attached to the house.

Mickey finished his chips and pushed his plate away. "Hand over the kitty, Jeff, I'll go and get the ice creams."

"Ice cream? You do realize it's below freezing out there—none too warm in here, come to that."

"What's that got to do with it?" As far as Mickey was concerned, ice cream was the only possible pudding, summer or winter.

"Give it to him, Jeff," said Liz. "He'd eat an ice cream cone in a snowstorm; I've seen him!"

Mickey went up to the café counter and studied the wall chart beside the refrigerator, working out just how big an ice cream he could afford.

The tall figure of Sir Jasper appeared in the doorway. "Ah, there you are. Do forgive my lack of hospitality, but I've been so rushed today." He waved to the lady behind the counter. "Give my young friends whatever they want, if you please. No charge, of course."

Mickey promptly ordered three large bunny-rabbits— ice cream cones with *two* chocolate wafers—and carried them back to the table. Sir Jasper insisted on paying for the three pies and chips as well. "After all, you are my guests, though I fear I'm a singularly neglectful host."

"That's all right," said Liz. "You've got a lot to worry about."

"I'm afraid I have. Mr. Chipsted, the builder, seems a most reliable fellow, but those men of his! Chipsted was saying it's hard to get good people these days. Mind you, he's obstinate enough himself, insists on tackling the foundation before the roof."

"Typical expert," said Jeff. "They always want to do things their way. No more trouble on the supernatural front?"

Sir Jasper looked around apprehensively. "Not as far as I know. Surely we're safe during the hours of daylight?"

"I hope so. Maybe we should take a look around, though?"

Still licking their ice creams, they strolled to the front of the house. Old Park House was open to the public all the year round, and naturally enough the biggest crowds came in the summer. But although it was December and icy cold, quite a few visitors had turned up, mostly the older and more serious types, who bought catalogs and made their way solemnly around the house.

Liz and Jeff finished their ice creams, grabbed Mickey, who'd finished long ago, gave him a brief spit-wash with his own grubby handkerchief, and followed Sir Jasper into the house and up the stairs.

There were about half a dozen visitors in the long gallery. Remembering Dan's words, Jeff studied them carefully, alert for suspicious characters.

There was the usual Japanese couple, intent on taking pictures of each other posed before every single picture in the gallery.

There were two old ladies in velvet hats, a schoolgirl with a notebook who looked as if she were on some holiday project, and an inconspicuous little man in a raincoat who looked rather like a retired schoolteacher. Like the Japanese, he was carrying a camera, though his stayed slung over his shoulder.

"As innocent-looking a bunch as you could wish to find," whispered Liz.

"Just what I was thinking. I think we'll just have to hang around until tonight."

"'Course we will," scoffed Mickey. "Ghosts don't walk till midnight, anyone knows that."

Liz shivered. "Let's go in the library then, there's a fire in there." She looked around. "Well, it may not be midnight, but it's dark enough." Winter shadows had gathered around the house.

They found the oak-paneled door, almost invisible in the oak-paneled wall, opened it, and went inside.

Jeff was last in line, and he was just about to close the door behind them when he heard a crash and a piercing scream. He whirled and saw that the black bust of the first Sir Jasper had fallen from its pedestal. Beside it the little Japanese woman was sobbing hysterically.

Sir Jasper came running up. "What's happened?"

The stocky Japanese husband was very angry. "Statue fall," he roared. "Nearly hit my wife. House not safe!"

"I'm most terribly sorry. I assure you the statue *was* safe. Perhaps it was disturbed by the building work. . . ."

The portrait of Sir Jasper suddenly dropped from the wall, hitting the ground with a bang.

This time the schoolgirl screamed, and the elder of the two old ladies promptly had hysterics.

Only the little man in the raincoat remained calm. In a surprisingly deep and authoritative voice he shouted: "Nobody must move. There is great danger here, great evil. I can sense it."

There was a moment of silence, broken only by the quiet sobbing of the Japanese woman.

The middle one of the gallery's three long windows exploded with a shattering crash.

7

The Ghost Hunter

Suddenly all the lights went out. A cold wind rushed in from the outside, there were sobs, shouts, cries of alarm. People began rushing about, bumping into each other, and there was another crash as another of the statues toppled over.

Only the little man in the raincoat remained calm. "Please, all of you, remain quite still. We can defeat the evil if we unite our wills. I ask you all to pray, to whatever God you believe in. If you have Bibles, crosses, holy relics of any kind, produce them."

One of the old ladies began mumbling a prayer, and the Japanese man began a deep soft chant. Liz fingered the gold cross on her bracelet. The real surprise was Mickey, who began singing 'While Shepherds Watched' in a surprisingly good soprano. Unfortunately, in his excitement he sang the version he and his friends always sang at the back of the choir:

"While shepherds washed their socks by night
All seated round the tub
A bar of Sunlight soap came down
And they began to scrub."

Despite this unauthorized version the combination of Mickey's singing and the assorted prayers did the trick. Or something did, anyway. The lights came on.

Once again the little man in the raincoat took command. In a firm voice he said, "I think the danger is over now. Nevertheless, I advise you all to go home as quickly as possible."

White-faced and silent, the visitors began filing out of the gallery and down the marble staircase. Sir Jasper followed, babbling explanations and apologies. But no one was listening. They just wanted to get out as soon as possible.

Mr. Chipsted appeared from somewhere in the nether regions, accompanied by a gorillalike workman. "What's going on here?"

Jeff collared him and took him aside. "There's been a kind of accident, and one of the gallery windows has been broken. Do you think you could rig up a tarpaulin or something? Otherwise it'll damage the paintings."

Grumbling, Mr. Chipsted went off to see about it.

Sir Jasper stood on the steps, Jeff, Liz and Mickey beside him, watching the shaken visitors hurry down the drive toward the little parking lot by the main entrance. There was a crashing of gears and a flashing of headlights, and soon the place was deserted.

Sir Jasper sighed. "Heaven knows what all those people will tell their friends. We can't hope to keep an event like this a secret. I shall have to close the place down."

"You would be well advised to do so," said a voice from behind them. They turned and saw the little man in the raincoat. He had obviously stayed behind in the hall when the rest had gone. "In my professional opinion—" Suddenly he broke off and shouted, "Look out!"

A stone flowerpot hurtled down from above and smashed on the steps a few feet away from Sir Jasper.

"Quick, inside, everyone," said the little man. He bustled them up the steps and into the hall. Shaken and trembling, Sir Jasper locked the door.

He turned to the little man. "I really don't know how to thank you enough. You prevented a dangerous panic upstairs, and now you seem to have saved my life."

"It's fortunate that I was here," said the little man simply. "There is a good deal of random violence in this kind of manifestation. It's not unknown for people to be seriously hurt, even killed."

Liz looked hard at him.

"You seem to know an awful lot about this kind of thing," she said. "And just now you were saying something about your *professional* opinion."

Mickey joined in the questioning. "Just who are you anyway? What are you doing here?"

The little man said quietly, "I am here purely by chance—a very fortunate chance, I might add. My name is Henry Pearce. You might call me a professional ghost hunter."

Sometime later they were all having tea by a roaring fire in Sir Jasper's study. Hot tea and buttered muffins had done a great deal to restore their spirits. But everyone was conscious of the cold and darkness outside the cozy, well-lit room. Uneasily Liz wondered if some evil force was still lurking in the big old house, biding its time, waiting until midnight.

Liz's nerves, like everyone else's, had been badly shaken by recent events. Like most people she was more or less skeptical about supernatural forces. But how else could you explain what they had just seen? She took a swig of tea and tried to fight off a feeling of rising panic.

Mr. Pearce wasn't helping much. In a quiet, reasonable voice he was telling of strange and horrifying events that had happened in haunted houses all over England. Strange moanings in the night, mysterious footsteps, sensations of unearthly chilling cold. Headless apparitions, bloodstains in floorboards that wouldn't go away, objects whizzing through the air of their own accord.

He told them about Borley Rectory, the most famous haunted house in England. "A phantom nun haunted the Rectory grounds—she often used to peer in at the windows and frighten visitors. A ghostly coach raced along the drive, strange voices moaned in the night. Writing appeared on the walls, a message saying, 'Marianne—please get help. . . .' "

Mickey's eyes were like saucers. "What happened, in the end?"

"The house burned to the ground," said Mr. Pearce solemnly. "They say ghosts gathered to watch the flames."

"Did anyone ever find out why all this was happening?" asked Jeff.

"Some years after the fire, a famous psychic investigator called Harry Price began excavating in the ruins.

When he was digging in the cellar he found the jawbone of a young woman."

"The phantom nun," whispered Liz.

Mr. Pearce nodded. "He gave the poor remnant Christian burial, and the hauntings came to an end."

There was an awed silence. Then Sir Jasper said, "That's a fascinating story, Mr. Pearce. Are you suggesting that the events here have some similar explanation?"

"I know something of the history of this place, Sir Jasper. That was why I decided to visit it. The building in itself is not particularly old, but it is built on the site of a much older one—a house mysteriously destroyed by the fire in which your ancestor, the first Sir Jasper, died."

Sir Jasper nodded, and Mickey said, "Come on then, Sir J, give us the full story."

Sir Jasper refilled all the teacups, passed around milk and sugar, and offered the last of the buttered muffins. Everyone was too full to take one except Mickey. He was full too, actually, but he took one anyway. There was something very comforting about buttered muffins.

Satisfied that everyone was comfortable, Sir Jasper sat back and began his story. "It's a pretty sordid tale, I'm afraid. My ancestor, who was the first baronet, was a thoroughly bad lot. He started as a minor politician, and got his baronetcy through some pretty murky services to the government. He was in on some big financial scandal, and got the baronetcy and a handsome sum of money as the price for keeping his mouth shut. Unfortunately, success went to his head, and he started trying to act like a real aristocrat, one of the old-time Regency rakes. In a few years he'd drunk and gambled most of the money away. He married a wealthy heiress, but before long he'd run through all her money too. Luckily she had the good sense to take her baby son and go back to her family."

Jeff felt himself being gripped by the story. "What about the night of the fire? What happened then?"

"Apparently by this time my wicked ancestor had only one friend left—if you can call him a friend. He was the Comte de Berger, descendant of a French family who'd got out of France with their money before the Revolution. They were both keen gamblers, and heavy drinkers too, I fear, and before very long they were both virtually destitute. Finally, Sir Jasper challenged his friend to one last gambling session."

Sir Jasper paused and moistened his throat with a swig of tea. "Sir Jasper insisted that the match be held here, at his house. The two friends met for dinner, there was a great deal of drinking, the servants were dismissed, and the two settled down to play."

Mickey was hopping with impatience. "Go on. Then what happened?"

"Nobody knows. Sometime in the night a fire broke out and the house burned to the ground. The Comte de Berger staggered from the blaze and died next day of his injuries. Sir Jasper's body was never found. There were all kinds of rumors, of course. Some people said Sir Jasper had murdered his friend and stolen the money, others that he had killed himself as well in drunken remorse."

Liz was listening in fascination. "I wonder what really happened."

Sir Jasper sighed. "I doubt if we shall ever know.

Eventually Sir Jasper's son, my grandfather, grew up, got in on the ground floor of the Industrial Revolution, restored the family fortunes, and built this house on the site of the old one."

"Using, in all probability, the foundations of the house that was destroyed," pointed out Mr. Pearce. "In my view, Sir Jasper, some such tragedy as you suggest undoubtedly occurred on that last fatal night. Sir Jasper was a violent, passionate man, and he would have been drinking heavily. Perhaps he lost his money, killed his friend in a fit of rage, and set the house on fire in a drunken attempt to conceal the crime, then accidentally died in the blaze he himself had caused." Mr. Pearce paused impressively. "What now seems certain is that his remains are still buried in the foundations of this house, and that his unhappy spirit is unable to rest."

Sir Jasper rubbed a worried hand over his high, bald forehead. "And I take it that you are suggesting . . ."

"Remember the case of Borley Rectory. We must find the poor fellow's remains and give them Christian burial. Only then will these terrible and dangerous events come to an end."

Dan Robinson wheeled the phone over to the bed and said, "Okay, Jeff, go on."

"I think that's about it. Mr. Pearce wants to hold some kind of séance here tonight—see if he can get in touch with the departed spirit."

"What does Sir Jasper say?"

"He's agreed to give it a try. I think the poor old boy's so desperate he'll try anything."

"What do you make of this chap Pearce?"

"He's pretty impressive," said Jeff. "Not what you'd expect a ghost hunter to be at all. Very quiet and detached, very professional." Jeff hesitated. "I think we might do well to leave this one to him, Dan. I mean, we're not doing too well so far, are we? I think we're a bit out of our depth."

It was a moment before Dan replied. "Give up, you mean?"

"What else can we do? You didn't see what happened in that gallery today, Dan. It was pretty terrifying, and it was only sheer luck no one got badly hurt. I don't mind taking on crooks, but we're not equipped to deal with the supernatural. Pearce is, or at least he seems to be, and as far as I'm concerned, he's welcome to it." There was an edge of tension in Jeff's voice that sounded very unlike him, and Dan realized that his stolid friend was close to panic.

"Look, Jeff, just stick it out for tonight, okay? Keep together, don't take any risks, see what happens at this séance. I should be out of here tomorrow. We can talk it all over and decide then."

"All right," said Jeff reluctantly. "Since we're all here anyway."

"That's the idea. I'll give you a call in the morning."

They said their good-byes, and Dan hung up.

He sat on the edge of his bed for a moment, staring at the telephone.

Dan slipped off the bed and began marching up and down the little room in sheer frustration. Everything was happening at Old Park House, and he was stuck here. For a moment he considered demanding his clothes and clearing out, but a brief wave of giddiness made him change his mind.

He got back on the bed and looked at his watch. It was half past five. He could hear the jingle and clink of the supper trolley. Everything happened early in hospitals, he thought irritably. Breakfast at crack of dawn, lunch at noon, supper at six, nice cup of cocoa at half past eight, and everyone tucked up cozily for the night.

Dan lay back on the bed and stared at the ceiling, going over events in his mind. It was one of the most frustrating cases he had ever tackled, nothing to get a grip on, and now it seemed that the case was being taken out of his hands altogether.

Dan scowled, trying to ignore the throbbing in his head. As far as he was concerned, reason was still the governing force in the universe, and he wasn't about to give up because of a few bumps in the night.

He tried to comfort himself with one of the most famous sayings of his beloved Sherlock Holmes. How did it go? "Once you have eliminated the impossible, whatever remains, *however improbable,* must be the truth." Something like that, anyway.

But suppose when you had eliminated the impossible —the only thing that remained was a malignant ghost?

8

The Séance

Jeff and Mickey wrestled the table through the door and set it down in the center of the library. "There," puffed Jeff. "Will that do?"

Mr. Pearce was busily sorting through the contents of a heavy wooden suitcase that he had fetched from his car. He straightened up and looked at the table. It was small and round, with a supporting pedestal in the center, and had a highly polished surface. Mr. Pearce had been very definite about the kind of table he wanted, and it had taken Jeff and Mickey quite a while to find exactly the right one in the furniture-filled rooms above, and longer still to wrestle it down the stairs and into the library.

"Excellent," said Mr. Pearce. "Exactly what we need."

Liz wondered what all these preparations were in aid of, but didn't like to ask.

Mickey, however, had no such inhibitions. "What's it for, then, the table? What are we going to do?"

"We shall attempt to communicate with the spirits of the dead."

"With an old table? How?"

"You'll see, my boy, you'll see."

Mr. Pearce went back to his case and went on

assembling his equipment, which seemed to consist of a strange assortment of electronic odds and ends.

Unabashed, Mickey peered over his shoulder. "What's this for?"

"Psychic research is a scientific business these days. These are scientific instruments. I assembled most of them myself."

"What do they do?"

"All kinds of things. There's a voice-operated tape recorder, an automatic camera, devices to record temperature and air pressure."

Mr. Pearce's raincoat lay on a chair, with the camera case he'd been carrying on top of it. "You're well off for cameras," said Mickey. "This one looks neat!"

He reached out to pick up the little case, but Mr. Pearce snatched it away. "Don't touch that, there's a good little fellow. It's a very expensive camera, and it's very delicate."

Jeff hauled Mickey to one side. "Leave the poor bloke alone, can't you? You can see he's busy."

"Only asking, wasn't I?" said Mickey, aggrieved. "How'm I going to learn anything, if I don't ask? Might want to be a spook chaser myself when I grow up."

"If you grow up," growled Jeff. "You're more likely to be a spook yourself."

Sir Jasper bustled into the room, agitated as usual. "I've just seen Mr. Chipsted and his men off the premises. He's promised to repair the gallery window tomorrow, *if* he can get hold of the glass. They've rigged a tarpaulin over it for the moment. Of course I suppose that will delay things even more now!"

Not for the first time, Jeff thought that with all the time Sir Jasper spent supervising everyone, he might just as well get a tool kit and tackle the whole job himself.

"Did you set the alarms?"

"I'm just going to do it now." Sir Jasper went over to the little control panel and set the main switch. Immediately the diagram of the house lighted up, a warning light blinking to show the broken window. Jeff looked skeptically at it. Theoretically, the window aside, the place was now sealed off from all intruders. Still, perhaps it wasn't fair to expect a burglar alarm to keep out a ghost. He looked at Mr. Pearce. "What do we do now, then?"

"First I shall assemble these various devices of mine at strategic points about the house. Places where there have been previous manifestations. Then we shall wait."

"Wait for what?" asked Liz uneasily.

"For midnight."

Mickey gulped. "What happens then?"

"We shall hold a séance. I happen to be an experienced medium." Mr. Pearce looked around benignly. "With your help, I shall make an attempt to communicate with the unhappy, tormented spirit that is haunting this house."

"What's the point of that?" asked Mickey. "I thought we wanted to get rid of it, not start having chats with it."

"So we do. But in order to lay the ghost to rest, we must find out what it wants."

Dan was just beginning to doze off when he heard a familiar voice outside his room. "Never you mind if it is well past visiting time, young lady. I'm the law, and like you, we work around the clock. Now, why don't you just stop fussing, and go and get us a nice cup of tea?"

A thin, sharp-faced young man in a shabby raincoat marched briskly into the room and perched on the end of the bed. "Hello, young Robinson. I hear you've been mixing with the spirit world? Must have been a pretty solid spook."

Delighted, Dan sat up. Detective Sergeant Day, known to his friends as "Happy Day," was an old friend of his, and he was touched that the young detective had taken the trouble to come and see him, particularly since Day, like most police detectives, was always frantically overworked. "Hello, Happy. Where's Fred Summers? I should have thought he'd have been around with a bunch of grapes by now."

Detective Sergeant Summers was Day's colleague, no friend to the Irregulars. He disapproved of kids' getting mixed up in crime, and disapproved even more strongly when they had the cheek to do it successfully.

Day grinned. "He's too busy to come, but he did send a message."

"What?"

"He said be sure to stay in the hospital and have a nice long rest—the longer the better!" Day changed his tone. "What's been going on at Old Park House? We had a couple of complaints this afternoon. Two old girls in hysterics, and a Japanese gent carrying on alarmingly. I couldn't get much sense out of any of 'em; I guessed you'd be mixed up in it somewhere. I called you up, and your mum told me you were in here."

"Not just visiting the sick after all, then? You've come to pick my brains."

"That's right. The poor dim, baffled copper comes to

ask the advice of the brilliant consulting detective." Day had never really got on with the Sherlock Holmes stories. He objected strongly to the way in which the police were always portrayed as nitwits. "Go on, then, Sherlock. Baffle me!"

"I only wish I could," said Dan ruefully. "I'm the one that's baffled at the moment."

He gave Day a complete account of the whole business, starting with the haunting of Sir Jasper, the vigil that had landed him in the hospital, giving Jeff's account of the events of the afternoon. "You'll have to talk to Jeff if you want it first hand, but that's exactly what he told me."

To Dan's surprise, the sharp-faced nurse came in with two cups of tea. "I shouldn't be doing this, really . . ."

Day took the tea from her. "Thanks, love, you're a sweetheart." The nurse went out giggling and Day caught Dan's eye. "Can't help it if I'm irresistible, can I?" He passed a cup over to Dan. "It's a funny business this, young Robinson. What do you make of it?"

"What I always did—someone's trying to scare Sir Jasper away. They tried a bit of midnight haunting, and when that didn't work they had another try when there were visitors, to make a public scandal so he'd have to close the place."

"But—" began Day.

"Never mind about but," yelled Dan. "I know all about the buts. The place is protected by an ultramodern alarm system, recently checked over by the man who installed it. Most of the time it's swarming with Mr. Chipsted and his merry band of builders, who've searched the place from top to bottom without finding anything or anyone suspicious. No secret passages, no lurking figures, no hidden mechanisms, nothing! Now, to top it all, we've got a professional ghost hunter, I beg his pardon, a psychic-research investigator, on the job, and he can't find any signs of fakery either!"

"All right, all right," said Day soothingly. "Here, drink up your tea, it'll calm you down." Dan reached for his tea and Day went on. "Look at it this way: there are only two chances. Either it's fakery, or it's genuine spooks. Now if it is spooks, there's nothing you or I can do, we'll just have to bow out gracefully, and leave it to this psychical-research bloke. So let's assume it's fakery. Never mind *how* for the moment, what about the *why?* What's the motive?"

"That's obvious, isn't it?" said Dan more calmly. "Someone thinks there's something valuable at Old Park House."

Day groaned. "Not another masterpiece! I mean, one turning up is bad enough, but two's pushing it a bit."

Dan shook his head. "I don't think it can be another painting. After the first one was found, Sir Jasper had everything in the place checked by Rundles, the art people, and they said there was nothing worth more than a few hundred pounds."

"That's what they said," repeated Day, with a detective's automatic suspicion. "Suppose they did find something valuable, and decided to say nothing and knock it off later."

"We went into all that when the first painting was stolen. Rundle and Son are a couple of pompous twits, but they're too snobbish to be dishonest, and too rich." Dan finished his tea. "I reckon whatever the something is, it must be hard to get at in some way."

"So—someone, we don't know who, is getting into the house, we don't know how, faking ghosts to scare off Sir Jasper, so they can search for something valuable, we don't know what, hidden somewhere inaccessible, we don't know where! Marvelous! Where do we go from there?"

"I'm not going anywhere, am I?" said Dan ruefully. "They insist on keeping me here till they're sure I haven't got concussion. You, on the other hand, are a free agent, with all the resources of our wonderful British police force at your command."

"And a case load so high I can't see over the top of my desk. I can't even put this one on the list, can I? There's been no crime reported."

"You've had a complaint from an angry Japanese tourist, haven't you? For all you know, the fate of the British Tourist Industry is in your hands."

"All right, all right. What do you want me to do?"

"Check!" said Dan explosively. "Check up on everyone involved. Check on Shepherd, the burglar-alarm bloke. Check on Mr. Chipsted the builder, Mr. Pearce the ghost hunter. You might just as well check on Rundles, too, though I doubt if it'll do any good."

"And what will you be doing, while I'm spending my valuable time and the taxpayers' money on a wild-ghost chase?"

"Thinking! I'm not giving up on this one, whatever anyone says. I've got a score to settle."

"That crack on the nut, you mean?" Day looked at the chamber pot and grinned. "I can see why you're up in arms about it. I mean, savage dwarves with blowpipes and poison snakes down the bellrope is one thing, but I bet Old Sherlock never got himself laid out with an antique potty!"

Dan looked thoughtfully at the old chamber pot. "You've just given me an idea. There's something else you can do for me."

When Detective Sergeant Day left the hospital a short time later, he was carrying, with some embarrassment, a large newspaper-wrapped parcel.

Liz, Jeff, and Mickey, Sir Jasper and Mr. Pearce were all seated around the little polished table. Their hands rested lightly on the surface, fingertips touching.

It was five minutes to midnight.

They had been sitting silent like this for about ten minutes, although it seemed much longer. Mr. Pearce had insisted on setting things up in good time. It was important that their minds should be calm and relaxed, he explained.

Liz was feeling anything but calm. Her arms were aching from the strain of maintaining the position, and somehow she felt bored and frightened at the same time.

Jeff's arms were aching too. He was trying to take his mind off the ache by going over the events of the afternoon. He had followed Mr. Pearce about the gallery, watching him set up his various detection devices, until Pearce had politely but firmly requested to be left alone. "The mechanisms are delicate, you understand, and the sensation of being continually overlooked . . ."

Jeff smiled to himself. Pearce was a decent old stick, but he obviously wasn't used to kids. Jeff noticed he still had his camera around his neck, as if determined to keep it away from Mickey's prying fingers.

Mickey himself was fidgeting restlessly on his seat. Perpetual motion was Mickey's style, it was torture for him to sit still for one minute, let alone ten, and the plain wooden chair was proving hard on his bony bottom.

Sir Jasper sat pale and tense, eyes half closed. Only Mr. Pearce looked calm and relaxed, staring raptly through half-closed eyes at the tiny table lamp in the center of the table. Suddenly he raised his head and said softly, "Something approaches—something evil. I can feel it."

Liz found herself shivering.

In a calm, almost hypnotic voice, Mr. Pearce said, "Is someone there? Please, give one knock for yes, two for no. Is anyone there?"

The sound of a single loud knock came from the table.

9

The Murderous Ghost

Everyone jumped—that is, everyone except Mr. Pearce, who said calmly, "Are you a departed spirit?"

Another knock for yes.

"Are you the spirit of the first Sir Jasper Ryde?"

A single knock again.

"Have you a message for someone here?"

Another knock.

"Is it for me?"

Two sharp knocks for no.

"For one of the children?"

Again two knocks.

"Is it for your descendant—for Sir Jasper Ryde?"

One single knock—very loud.

There was a pause, as if Mr. Pearce were collecting his thoughts. Then he said, "Do you wish your mortal remains to be found, and given Christian burial?"

One knock.

"Do you wish your descendant to do this?"

There came a string of no's—double knocks, all very loud.

"Do you wish him to stay here while it is done?"

More double knocks.

"You wish him to go—and to return when you are at peace?"

This time there came a whole series of single knocks, very definite yeses.

"If he does this, will you depart and leave us in peace?"

Another yes knock.

"And if he does not?"

There were no more knocks, but suddenly the table began rocking to and fro beneath their hands. They tried to hold it down, but it rocked harder, harder, swaying backward and forward until it overturned with a crash, smashing the lamp. They all jumped to their feet.

"Stay very still, all of you," whispered Mr. Pearce. "The departed spirit is angry—there is danger."

No one moved.

Mr. Pearce moved toward the door to the gallery and opened it.

They stared out into the long, darkened room. There was a strange flapping sound. Jeff jumped, then realized it was the tarpaulin over the broken window, flapping in the icy night winds.

A glowing shape appeared at the far end of the gallery. It was a man in old-fashioned dress, with a face uncannily like Sir Jasper's own.

Mr. Pearce put a hand on Sir Jasper's arm. "Please, don't go out there, I beg of you. It's too dangerous."

Sir Jasper shook off the hand. "Since my ancestor's been good enough to pay me a visit, I'd better go and see what he wants."

As he stepped out into the gallery, the apparition faded and there was a whizzing sound, followed by a thud.

Jeff ran into the gallery. Sir Jasper was standing very still, just outside the door, his face white with shock. A spear was embedded deep in the oak paneling behind him.

Jeff glanced at the still-quivering spear, and sprinted the length of the gallery as if he were trying to break the hundred-yards record. That spear had been hurled just seconds ago, and the thrower couldn't be far away. He shot through the door at the far end of the staircase and found himself out on the landing.

There was no one there.

He looked up and down the staircase. No one there, and no sound of movement.

He heard Liz's voice behind him. "Jeff, come back!" He turned and ran back into the gallery.

Someone was moving in the semidarkness, and Jeff tripped over something hard and heavy. Suddenly the lights came on and he saw that he'd tripped over Mr. Pearce's wooden case—and over Mr. Pearce.

Pearce picked himself up and helped Jeff to his feet. "This is where the spear came from." He indicated a display of ancient weapons on the wall.

Sir Jasper came along the gallery, the spear in his hand. "It's a Zulu assegai—belongs just there." Reaching up, he fitted the spear back into the holding clips. "My worthy ancestor seems to have it in for me, doesn't he?"

Liz and Mickey came up. "Jeff, are you all right?" asked Liz.

Jeff nodded silently.

"Did you see anyone?" asked Mickey eagerly.

"No. There was no one there."

"What about that spear?" demanded Mickey. "It took Sir J all this time to get it out of the wall. Somebody chucked it!"

"The spear was propelled by psychic energy," announced Mr. Pearce calmly. "In a few moments I shall give you proof. If you will all be kind enough to return to the study, I should like to check my instrument readings undisturbed."

They all filed back to the library, and Mickey said cheerfully, "Time for the midnight feast, isn't it?"

Sir Jasper's housekeeper had left them a kind of picnic hamper.

Liz groaned. "Trust you to think of food at a time like this. I'm too scared to eat."

They unpacked the basket all the same, though, and found mounds of chicken sandwiches, a big thermos of cocoa, and a pile of mugs and plates.

Liz poured the cocoa and Jeff dished out the sandwiches, and when Mr. Pearce came back he found them all calmly tucking in. It seemed they weren't too scared to eat after all; in fact, the excitement seemed to have given everyone an appetite.

Refusing cocoa, Mr. Pearce said, "I have checked my instrument readings, and the results are quite positive. At the time of the manifestation there was a sharp drop in temperature and a sudden rise in air pressure—both established evidence of psychic activity."

"That spear was evidence enough for me," said Sir Jasper. "What do we do now?"

"I should seriously advise you to leave here as soon as possible, Sir Jasper," said Mr. Pearce solemnly. "At least until your ancestor's remains have been found and properly buried."

"Why should this spook have it in for Sir J?" asked Mickey. "I mean, he is one of the family."

"The spirit is tormented by shame and guilt. It is possible he feels that until he is laid to rest, the present Sir Jasper is in some way usurping his place. Remember, we are dealing with the spirit of a violent and irrational man, and earthbound spirits often retain, and indeed intensify, the characteristics they exhibited in life."

"But if I do leave, who will supervise the search for my ancestor's remains? I can scarcely leave it to Mr. Chipsted—after all, it hardly comes within the boundaries of normal building work." Sir Jasper looked thoughtfully at Mr. Pearce. "I don't suppose that by any chance you might be prepared . . ."

Mr. Pearce looked dubious. "There are a great many calls on my time, Sir Jasper . . ." He paused. "However, in a case of such extraordinary interest as this—it would make a splendid final chapter for my book! Yes, I think I may say that if you need my services, they are at your disposal."

"That's very kind of you." Sir Jasper coughed. "I should of course expect to reimburse you for your valuable time."

"No, no, Sir Jasper, there can be no question of that. The knowledge that one more unhappy spirit has been laid to rest will be reward enough. Your builder and his men can perfectly well carry out the actual physical side of the work, so my task would be merely advisory."

Mickey leaned over to Jeff. "Listen to 'em. They

sound like something out of those classic serials on the television!"

Jeff shushed him.

Liz said, "Don't you think we ought to discuss it with Dan, Sir Jasper? I mean, you did ask him for help, and he did get clunked. Now he's in the hospital, not knowing what's going on."

"Quite right, my dear," said Sir Jasper. "I shall go and see him tomorrow." He turned to Mr. Pearce. "I may well decide to accept your most generous offer. But first I must talk it over with Dan Robinson."

Mr. Pearce got to his feet. "You must do as you think best, Sir Jasper, of course. But I advise you not to delay your decision too long. May I remind you that you have had a number of narrow escapes? While you remain here you are a focal point for danger, not only to yourself, but to those around you. These children, for example."

"I thought it was only Sir Jasper the spook had it in for?" asked Mickey cheekily. "Why should the rest of us be in any danger?"

Mr. Pearce looked solemnly at him. "You saw how close that spear passed to Sir Jasper! Suppose you had been standing next to him?"

"Would have gone right over my head, wouldn't it?"

"And when the flowerpot crashed down?" Pearce turned to Sir Jasper. "These children are too young to realize the risks they run. Random psychic violence often hits unintended targets."

Sir Jasper said worriedly, "I must admit that hadn't occurred to me. I should hate to be the cause of anyone else being harmed. I'll think it over very carefully, Mr. Pearce."

Mr. Pearce bowed. "I must be going. If I may, I'll call around tomorrow and we can discuss the matter further."

Sir Jasper showed Mr. Pearce out, locked up behind him, and came back to the study. He looked around at the others. "It's very late, and you must all be exhausted. My housekeeper has prepared beds for you all—"

"No thanks," said Liz firmly. "I don't want a strange bed tonight. We'll just camp out in here till morning if you don't mind."

And so they did. Liz stretched out on the sofa, Jeff and Sir Jasper took the armchairs, and Mickey curled up with cushions on the thick rug, wishing he had Baskerville to hug.

"Do you think anything more will happen tonight?" asked Liz sleepily.

Sir Jasper made up the fire and settled back in his chair. "I don't think so. It seems to restrict itself to one manifestation a night."

"Maybe it's worn out," said Jeff sleepily. "I know I am."

One by one the three Irregulars dropped off. Only Sir Jasper stayed awake all night, gazing into the dying fire, waiting for the gray light of dawn to show through the chink in the curtains.

10
Blind Alley

"Don't do it, Sir Jasper!" said Dan Robinson explosively. "This chap Pearce may be genuine, but he's advising you to do exactly what someone wants—to get out and leave them a clear field."

Dan was sitting up in bed having midmorning tea and cookies. After driving the other Irregulars home, Sir Jasper had come straight around to see Dan.

Sir Jasper said. "You're still convinced someone wants me to leave the house? What someone—and why?"

Dan repeated his theory—that something valuable was hidden in Old Park House, and that someone wanted to drive Sir Jasper away so as to have time to discover it and take it away.

Sir Jasper took all this in. "Do you really think Mr. Pearce may be involved?"

Dan shrugged. "I don't know. Anything's possible."

"The hauntings all started before Pearce appeared," pointed out Sir Jasper. "What's more, I offered him a fee for his services and he turned it down. Even if I accept his suggestion, there'll still be Mr. Chipsted to keep an eye on things."

Dan nodded wearily. There was something curiously baffling about this case, he thought. Somehow his mind couldn't seem to get a grip on it. Maybe it was that knock on the head. The who, the how, and the why of it all seemed to be eluding him.

Sir Jasper looked sympathetically at him. "Aren't you being a little obstinate, Dan? First you thought I was imagining everything. Even when you saw the ghost yourself, you were just as certain that the whole thing was a fake—despite the fact that there are no obvious suspects, no clear motive, and no way that any intruders could get into the house without being detected by the burglar alarm. Isn't it possible that we really are faced with the supernatural?

Dan shook his head obstinately, convinced that there was an explanation, if only he could find it.

Sir Jasper asked after Dan's injuries—the doctor was still being exasperatingly vague about when he could go home—and rose to leave. "One thing Pearce said did impress me, Dan. I don't mind running risks myself, but I've no right to endanger those around me. Your three friends, for instance, and the members of the public. I'm going to close the house to visitors, at least for a while."

"All right. I can understand how you feel. But please, don't move out yourself without letting me know."

"As soon as I reach a decision, you'll be the first to hear," promised Sir Jasper. "By the way, I brought you this." He handed Dan the leather-bound volume of *A Study in Evil,* and went away.

Dan pushed his tray aside and lay staring into space. He knew something crooked was going on at Old Park House. He knew it. But how could he prove it, when he was stuck in this wretched hospital? Maybe Detective Sergeant Day would come up with something.

As if in answer to his thoughts, the telephone rang, and Dan reached out and grabbed it. It was Day. "I've done that bit of checking up for you, Dan."

"And?"

"Nothing. Nothing all the way down the line. I rang up old Rundle first of all, and asked if there was any chance of anything valuable being in the place."

"What did he say?"

Day gave a passable imitation of Mr. Rundle's pompous tones. "Really, officer, do you imagine I didn't think of that after finding a hitherto unknown painting by Constable? My staff examined every single item in that house, from cellar to attic. There are quite a few bits of interesting Victoriana, but nothing worth more than a few hundred pounds. And there are definitely no undiscovered masterpieces, large or small."

"Terrific," said Dan wearily. "What about the others?"

"Shepherd Electronics seem to be a thoroughly respectable little firm, very go-ahead, branching out into all kinds of things, not just burglar alarms."

"And Chipsted?"

"Respected local tradesman, noted for the high quality of his craftsmanship. Been in the building trade for years."

"What about Mr. Pearce?"

"I called the Occult Research Society. Mr. Henry Pearce is a most respected investigator, hates any kind of fakery, and has exposed a number of frauds. The word in the business is that if Pearce says it's a ghost, it's a genuine spook. Sorry, Dan, your three suspects are all model citizens. I'd give up this particular ghost if I were you. Find yourself a nice simple burglary."

"Maybe I will. Thanks for trying, anyway."

The morning dragged on. The nurse cleared the tray and straightened the bed. The doctor called, examined him, and said he could go home "soon," aggravatingly refusing to be any more precise.

His mother popped in on the way to one of her innumerable social-work committee meetings, bringing the traditional basket of fruit. Apparently everything was okay at home except that Baskerville was off his food and spent most of the day sitting on the corner of the street, waiting for Dan's return.

Finally the Irregulars arrived, Jeff, Liz and Mickey, all rather red-eyed after two nights in succession without proper sleep. Dan insisted on a second account of the events of the previous night, even though he'd heard it all once from Sir Jasper.

He made each of them go through it in turn, trying to establish exactly what had happened, where everyone had been, and what they'd seen. It was infuriating, having to work at second hand like this, but after blending all the accounts together, Dan thought he had a pretty clear picture of what had happened.

When they'd all finished, he told them of Day's checkup on Chipsted, Shepherd, and Pearce, and the negative results.

Jeff stared glumly at him. "Blind alleys wherever we turn. I vote we pack it in."

Liz was pessimistic too. "You must admit it's a bit of a nonevent, Dan. No motive, no method, no suspects—no real crime!"

"What about chucking spears at Sir Jasper?" said

Mickey indignantly. "Or bonking Dan with a jerry, come to that. Don't you call that a crime?"

"Tell you what. We'll get Day to take out a warrant and arrest the ghost," said Jeff. "Malicious damage and grievous bodily harm. Be a sensation in court."

As usual when lost for words, Mickey took refuge in action. He grabbed an apple from Dan's fruit basket and threw it at Jeff's head. Jeff caught the apple neatly and began to eat it. Mickey grabbed a banana for himself, and Liz started work on the grapes.

Dan looked disgustedly at them. "Everybody all right, then? Shall I ring for tea?" He took a banana for himself. "Now listen, all of you. Mickey's quite right."

" 'Course I am," said Mickey, though he wasn't really sure what he was right about. "Tell 'em, Dan."

"You're all being thrown by the supernatural element. Let's say this was an ordinary robbery, something stolen from a bank or a museum, with a super alarm system. We wouldn't be worried by the fact that nobody could have got in and we'd no idea who the thieves were. We'd just accept that the impossible had happened, and get on with investigating it."

"Yes, but then we'd have a crime to investigate," objected Jeff. "Something definite, something that had actually happened. Like Liz says, we haven't even got a crime."

"Oh, yes, we have," said Dan quietly. "As a matter of fact, I think we've got two. Only one happened hundreds of years ago and the other hasn't happened yet!"

Jeff said, "All right, Sherlock. Explain!"

"I'm convinced that what's happening now is linked

with what happened all those years ago. The death of the first Sir Jasper, the fire . . . somehow those events are reaching forward through time, causing something else to happen. All this spook stuff is only paving the way."

There was an uneasy silence. Then Liz said, "That's marvelous, a crime in the past and a crime in the future. How are we going to investigate them? Where do we start?"

"In the here and now, of course; that's all we can do."

"How?" said Jeff. "What do we investigate?"

"Shepherd, Chipsted, and Pearce. Sounds like an old-fashioned firm of lawyers, doesn't it?"

"Day's already checked up on them, and he couldn't find anything."

"That doesn't mean there's nothing to find. Day's snowed under with work, remember? Like all the police. He probably spent about ten minutes investigating all three of them. That's where we come in. We're private detectives, like Sherlock Holmes. We can pick and choose our cases, spend time on tracking down clues."

"We haven't got any clues!"

"Then go out and find me some!"

"That's the spirit," said Mickey. "What do you want us to do?"

"Investigate," said Dan simply. "Take one of 'em each. You take Mr. Pearce, the medium, Liz. Jeff, your dad's the do-it-yourself king, you take Mr. Chipsted the builder. Mickey, that leaves Mr. Shepherd the burglar-alarm man for you."

"Okay," said Mickey confidently. "I'm the technological expert around here anyway."

Actually there was a surprising amount of truth in Mickey's claim. He had a quick brain and nimble fingers, and he soon picked up the workings of anything that interested him. His knowledge of radio-controlled model airplanes was unrivaled in the entire school.

Jeff was still feeling balky. "Investigate what, Dan? I mean, you can't really call any of them suspects; we've no evidence they've done anything."

"Then find some. Poke about, sniff around, make a nuisance of yourselves. If one of them is mixed up in anything shady, it'll show up somewhere."

"You must admit, Dan, it's all a bit vague," said Liz. "We don't even know what you're looking for."

"Anything! Anything at all. Reactions, for a start. The guilty one won't react like the others, he'll think you're on to him even if you're not."

"That's great," said Jeff. "So we lurk about, drop a few mysterious hints, and whoever gets bashed over the head has found the one we're looking for!"

"That's a very good point, Jeff. Now, listen, all of you. Make sure someone knows where you are, stay in public places . . . especially you, Mickey. And check in with me regularly."

Mickey said, "And while we're out slogging, you'll be lolling back here eating grapes, I suppose?"

"Wrong—for a start, Liz has finished them. Anyway, I shall occupy myself with some serious research. While you're all chasing the future crime, I shall be buried in the past."

He picked up the thick leather-bound volume from the bedside table.

"What's that?" asked Liz.

"Sir Jasper brought it over for me." Dan held up the book *A Study in Evil.* "The story of the first Sir Jasper Ryde. The one whose ghost has been giving us all this trouble . . ."

11
Hunt for Shadows

Jeff, Liz, and Mickey paused irresolutely on the hospital steps and stood looking at each other.

"Well, better get on with it," said Jeff at last.

Liz nodded. "I suppose so."

Both voices showed an equal lack of enthusiasm. Maybe the weather was depressing them, thought Liz. It was one of those indeterminate winter days, cold, but not cold enough to promise snow, gray, but not cloudy enough for rain.

"You're a fine pair," jeered Mickey. "Anyone'd think you were going to a funeral, not an investigation."

Jeff looked at Mickey, envying his enthusiasm. Mickey was convinced he was about to embark on a thrilling adventure, make dramatic discoveries, and finish in a blaze of glory with his name and picture in the paper. Jeff, on the other hand, felt he was about to go and ask a lot of stupid questions to some probably quite innocent strangers, and finish up covered in nothing more than confusion.

Liz obviously felt the same. "You know, I've just realized something. We don't know where we're going!"

"You're telling me!"

"I don't mean in the investigation, I mean literally. Addresses, and stuff like that."

Jeff considered. "We could go back and ask Dan."

"Let's go back to Old Park House," suggested Liz. "Sir Jasper will have the information, and we can see what's going on at the same time. Okay, Mickey?"

"As long as we get on with *something!*" Mickey unpadlocked his bike from the hospital railings, swung a leg over the saddle, and zoomed off up the hill as if he were on the last leg of the Tour de France bicycle race.

Jeff and Liz unlocked their bikes and followed at a more sedate pace, weaving in and out of the slowly moving lines of traffic that blocked the narrow High Street.

As they turned into the driveway of Old Park House, Liz said, "I suppose Mickey's right, we are being a bit downbeat."

"I suppose so. But it's such a weird case, isn't it? Anyway, it's not the same without old Dan."

"He's still keen enough."

"I wonder if he's not being a bit too keen."

"How do you mean?"

"Well, he just won't give up, will he? No suspects, no crime, no clues, yet old Dan still keeps plugging away— and dragging us along with him."

"We can't let him down, though, can we? Especially now he's stuck in the hospital. I mean he's depending on us."

"We can't go hunting shadows forever either. I'll give it another day, but if we don't turn anything up between us, I'm packing it in."

By now they'd reached the front of the house, where Mickey was jumping up and down waiting for them.

"Come on, you two, what did you do, get off and push? Mr. Pearce is here now, talking to Sir Jasper."

As they got off their bikes, Sir Jasper and Mr. Pearce came down the steps. "I'm sorry, Mr. Pearce," Sir Jasper was saying distractedly, "but I still haven't made up my mind what to do for the best."

Mr. Pearce said disapprovingly, "I can only urge you not to delay too long. In my view things cannot go on as they are without some tragedy occurring. Not only you yourself, but innocent bystanders will be in danger until this business is resolved. And as far as my own services are concerned, Sir Jasper, I must press you for a decision by tomorrow. I have been asked to investigate a most interesting case of poltergeistic activity in Norfolk. I consider this affair more serious, and am prepared to give it priority—but I must know by tomorrow. I shall take the liberty of calling on you in the morning."

Ignoring the three Irregulars, Mr. Pearce marched stiffly to the Ford, got in, started the car, and drove sedately away.

Sir Jasper, distracted but polite as ever, said, "Now, my young friends, what can I do for you?"

Jeff told him about the three addresses they needed, and Sir Jasper scratched his head. "Shepherd Electronics and Mr. Chipsted are easy enough. But Mr. Pearce—do you know, I've no idea where he lives? He's always called on me, you see."

Liz saw her assignment vanishing under her eyes. With a hurried "Excuse me!" she jumped on her bike and pedaled furiously down the drive.

Sir Jasper stared after her in astonishment. "Dear me! Whatever can be the matter?"

"Don't worry," said Jeff soothingly. "If you'll just give us those addresses, we'll get out of your hair." He blushed, catching sight of Sir Jasper's gleaming bald pate. "Er, out of your way, I mean. Don't worry about Liz."

"She'll be back in a minute, anyway," said Mickey. "How's she going to follow a car on a bike?"

Liz was wondering exactly the same thing, as she shot down the drive. Suppose Mr. Pearce was already out of sight? The whole idea was crazy, really; it was just that she felt she had to do something.

But her luck was in. The drive of Old Park House led onto a busy main road, and emerging motorists had to wait for a while before some kindly fellow motorist would let them out. Kindly drivers were obviously in short supply this morning, and by the time she reached the front gates, the black Ford was just pulling out into the main traffic stream. Liz waited for a moment, and then followed.

For the moment at least her luck continued. The road past Old Park House was long and narrow, and sectioned off by frequent traffic lights and pedestrian crossings. Traffic was slow this morning, little more than a moving jam. Liz found it easy enough to keep just behind the black Ford—the problem was not to overtake it.

However, she knew this couldn't last. If the traffic flow cleared, or if Pearce turned off onto an empty road, the old Ford would just streak away from her.

Just at that moment she saw the Ford's indicator lights blink, signaling a left turn. The car turned, Liz followed, and found herself on a wide residential avenue, almost completely clear of traffic. The Ford accelerated into the distance, turned a corner and disappeared.

Liz drew into the curb with a sigh. Might as well turn back; she'd lost him for good now. Or had she? Pearce had turned off into an area known as The Suburb, and it was completely and utterly residential. No shops, no pubs, no cinemas, just rows and rows of neat little houses on peaceful tree-lined streets. It wasn't on the way to anywhere, it didn't offer any shortcuts—in fact, the only reason for going there was as either a resident or a visitor.

Taking her time, Liz rode off in the direction taken by the car.

For the next half hour she rode up and down the streets of The Suburb in a methodical search pattern, keeping an eye out for the black Ford. She was gambling not only that Pearce lived in The Suburb, but also that he parked his car in the street. Hopefully she rode up and down the various streets and at last her persistence paid off.

In a quiet tree-lined cul-de-sac, she saw the black Ford. It was standing at the curb outside a large and opulent villa. The villa was called Dunromin.

Liz stared at it in fascination. She'd never really believed places called Dunromin actually existed. Maybe the one next door was called Bideawee.

She stopped on the corner, considering her next move. Presumably Mr. Pearce was inside the house—there was plenty of room in the street, no reason for him to park anywhere but outside the house he was going inside. The trouble was, he was still in there. If she knocked at the door, he'd know at once that she'd followed him. What could she say? Liz realized she'd dashed off in such a hurry that she'd had no time to work out a cover story. Maybe she should just make a note of the address and come back later.

Her dilemma was resolved by the sudden opening of Dunromin's door. Mr. Pearce came out. Liz ducked behind a tree. He was in a hurry and obviously in something of a flap. He got into the car and drove away.

On a sudden impulse, Liz rode up to the house, parked her bike at the curb, locked it, and went up and knocked on Dunromin's door.

It opened with surprising suddenness, and Liz found herself facing a tall rather plumpish lady in a violently colorful silk dressing gown. She had bright-red hair piled high on top of her head, and she wore a good deal of makeup.

Liz blinked. "Is Mr. Pearce here, please?"

"You've just missed him, luv. He went out a minute ago."

"Oh, dear. I had a message for him. From Sir Jasper Ryde, at Old Park House."

As Liz had hoped, Sir Jasper's name made an impression. "You'd best come in." The woman had what Liz always thought of as a *Coronation Street* accent. She ushered Liz across a thickly carpeted hall, its walls covered with framed photographs, and into a large, gleaming, ultra-modern kitchen. The room was spotless, so much so that it looked curiously unlived in, like a display kitchen at an exhibition.

"Would you like a cup of tea, luv? You must be fair starved, day like this!"

"A cup of tea would be lovely, but I'm not hungry, honestly."

The woman chuckled. "I meant starved with cold, luv, not starved with hunger. I'll never get used to the way you folk talk down South.

"You're from the North then?" The woman was obviously a friendly, chatty soul, and Liz felt that the more questions she asked, the fewer she'd have to answer.

"That's right, luv, how ever did you guess? I'm Lanky, I am, and proud of it! Lancashire. Born and bred in Blackpool. Here, sit yourself down."

The woman ushered Liz to a seat in a breakfast alcove, and began bustling about the kitchen.

"How did you come to move down here then?"

"Well, it were my Billy, really. He always said, 'Gracie, one day we're going to sell up, move down South, and live like ladies and gentlemen.'" She filled a kettle and began setting out tea-things. "Sure enough, one day we did. Buy this house, move down here, and then what does the old fool do but catch the flu and pop off, leaving me stuck here on me own." She spoke with a sort of affectionate exasperation; as if her husband had died on purpose, to annoy her.

"What did you do in Blackpool?" Liz thought of the framed photographs in the hall, the woman's generally larger-than-life air, and made an intuitive guess she felt was worthy of Dan himself. "I know. You were a landlady. A theatrical landlady!"

"You're a sharp one, aren't you." The kettle had boiled by now, and the woman was pouring tea into a blue-and-white-striped pot. "One for each person, and one for the pot!" She poured on the boiling water. "There, we'll just let that mash a minute." Then she turned to Liz. "Famous in the profession, I was. Best digs in Blackpool."

Liz decided she'd better steer the conversation onto more useful lines. "Is that where you met Mr. Pearce?"

"Aye, that's right. Mind you, that wasn't his name then—he changed it for professional reasons. Poor little beggar, I always had a soft spot for him. I were flabbergasted when he turned up here. I only took him in for old times' sake, I'm retired really." She passed Liz a cup of tea and a tin of cookies. "Help yourself, luv, sugar if you want it. Now, what about this message of yours? This Sir Jasper having a party, is he?"

"A party?"

The woman rattled on. "He won't want to miss a good booking, he hasn't been doing too well lately, not if the amount of rent he owes me's any guide. When's it for, then? That is what you've come for, isn't it? To book him?"

"Book him? Are you telling me Mr. Pearce is in show business?"

"Well, of course he is." The woman took Liz's arm, and led her into the hall. She pointed to one of the gallery of signed framed photographs. "There he is."

Liz found herself looking at a very different Mr. Pearce. He was posing stiffly in evening dress and a long cloak, a top hat in one hand and a rabbit in the other.

The photograph was signed "To Mrs. Wagstaffe—from The Great Mysterioso."

Mickey leaped puffing from the top of the down escalator and straight into the arms of the ticket collector. "Gotcha! Where's your ticket?"

With an air of triumphant virtue, Mickey produced his ticket. Time was he hadn't been above ducking under the barrier without one, but now he was an Irregular, that was a thing of the past. Disappointed, the ticket collector let him go. "All right, but just remember in future the up escalator's for going up, and the down for going down, okay?"

Mickey ducked past him. "Didn't anyone ever tell you exercise is good for you?" There was a local map at the entrance to the tube station, and Mickey found the street he was looking for and headed toward it.

When Liz had failed to reappear, Jeff and Mickey had decided they'd better carry on with their own assignments.

Sir Jasper had given Mickey the address he needed, and since Shepherd Electronics was some way away in the city, Mickey had decided to go by Underground. The train had been nearly empty, and he had enlivened the journey by swinging from strap handle to strap handle like Tarzan, until an indignant guard had threatened to chuck him off.

The excitement of the journey over, Mickey turned his mind to a bit of serious detective work. Shepherd Electronics turned out to be a hangarlike building in a yard at the end of a cobbled alley. The gate was open, there was no one about, so naturally Mickey slipped inside. He was a great believer in direct action. The door to the building was open too. Cautiously Mickey slipped across the yard and went inside.

He found himself in Aladdin's cave.

The inside of the building was one enormous room, like a large garage, or a small aircraft hangar. Workbenches were spaced about the floor.

Suspended over the central and largest bench was the biggest and most elaborate spaceship model Mickey had ever seen in his life. Huge, white, and gleaming, covered with hatches and gunports and antennas, it looked like the product of a million model kits put together.

A couple of ray guns lay on the bench beneath it. Adjoining benches held parts of space suits, models of smaller spacecraft, lunar vehicles. On one of them lay what appeared to be the fanged head of a very nasty-looking monster.

Mickey moved closer to the big spaceship, staring up at it in admiration. Suddenly he heard a scuffling sound behind him. He turned. A werewolf jumped from behind one of the benches and rushed growling toward him.

12
The Magic Men

Mickey gave a yell of alarm. Instinctively he grabbed one of the ray guns from the bench, swung it around, and fired.

The gun gave a fierce electronic beep and shot out a ray of light. "Aaargh!" screamed the werewolf. It rolled around the floor clutching its stomach, gave a few spasmodic kicks, and went limp.

Mickey stared at the gun in his hands in consternation. The werewolf got up, pulled off its wolf mask and claws, and said approvingly. "Well, done, sonny. Most kids run a mile when I do that!"

Stripped of its trappings, the werewolf was revealed as a scrawny youth not much bigger than Mickey himself, though clearly several years older, with a wizened monkeylike face. "You're not supposed to be in here, you know!"

"I just wanted—"

"I know what you wanted, sonny, you wanted to see the models. You don't think you're the first kid we've had hanging around here, do you? Like flies they are, 'specially in the school holidays. You're lucky they're all around the pub, or you'd have copped a clip on the ear from old Harry."

Since he'd been presented with a ready-made cover

story, Mickey decided to go along with it. "Well, you can't blame anyone for wanting to have a look. You've got some marvelous stuff here."

The youth looked around the workshop with proprietary pride. "Not bad, is it?" He looked up at the giant model. "That's the Zargon Death Ship from *Horror in Outer Space*. It's all science fiction these days, isn't it?"

Mickey was baffled. "Is it?"

The youth nodded toward the werewolf mask. "Used to be all horror, didn't it? Werewolves, vampires, demons. Before that it was mostly war, Sten guns, tanks, Spitfires, gas masks. That was my favorite, really. Still, it'll come around again, that's what the boss says, anyway."

Mickey was beginning to wonder if he'd come to the wrong place. "That's Mr. Shepherd, is it, the boss?"

"That's right, old Baa-lamb. Not that he's much of a lamb, more of a wolf really."

"What about the burglar alarms?"

The youth looked blankly at him. "Burglar alarms?"

"That's right. Shepherd Security. 'Let Shepherds Watch by Night.' All the latest in sonic alarm devices."

"I reckon you've come to the wrong place, kid. We're special effects, not security. Though mind you . . ." He paused, as if remembering something.

"What?" asked Mickey eagerly.

"Well, old Baa-lamb was messing about with something in number-two shop a while ago. Something radio-controlled, I think. I know these bells kept going off. I thought it was one of those caper jobs—you know, jewel robberies and that." He looked keenly at Mickey, as if recognizing that there was more than casual curiosity involved in his questions. "What's it to do with you, anyway, thought you just wanted to see the spaceship models?"

"Oh, just asking," said Mickey vaguely. "Someone told me you did burglar alarms."

"Well, we don't, and you'd better hoppit. They'll all be back in a minute."

"They're back now," said a voice behind them.

Mickey turned.

Mr. Shepherd was standing in the doorway. "What's going on, Alfie? Running another of your tours, are you?"

"Just some kid hanging about to see the models, Mr. Shepherd."

"Well, chuck him out. I've told you before, this is a place of business, not a flippin' museum."

Alfie turned to Mickey, all his friendliness gone now the boss was back. "You heard what the boss, said, sonny. Hoppit!"

"All right, all right. I'm going."

Mickey headed toward the door. Unfortunately he had to pass right by Shepherd to go through it, and he was uncomfortably aware that the man was staring hard at his face. It was a while since they'd met at Old Park House though, so perhaps . . . Mickey was just sidling through the door when Shepherd grabbed him by the arm. "Hang on a minute. I know you. You're one of those nosy Baker Street Irregulars, aren't you? You were there at Old Park House."

"He was asking a lot of questions, Mr. Shepherd,"

said Alfie virtuously. "About burglar alarms and stuff."

"And of course you told him all he wanted to know." Still gripping Mickey's arm, Shepherd dragged him across the workshop and shoved him into a tiny office sectioned off in the far corner of the room. He pushed Mickey into a chair and stood over him threateningly. "Now then, what's all this about? Why've you come all the way down here nosing about?"

"Why shouldn't I?" said Mickey boldly. "Got something to hide, have you?"

Shepherd took a whiskey bottle and a glass from the desk and poured himself a drink. "You're trespassing on private property, you know. I could call the police."

"Go on then. Tell 'em you found a kid in your yard. Maybe they'll send around a squad car."

Shepherd glared furiously at him. "You could have a very nasty accident, you know. Lots of dangerous stuff around here, explosives, live electrical gear. Now, tell me what you're up to or . . ."

Mickey had been threatened by real villains in his time, and he wasn't easily frightened. "Or what? I suppose you're gonna strap me to the circular saw? Or shoot laser beams up me trouser legs like in that Bond film?"

There was a strangled chuckle from behind them, and Shepherd swung around furiously. Alfie was watching them from the doorway. Shepherd promptly gave him a clip on the ear. "There's something to laugh about! I'm going to my office to make a phone call. You get back to work—and keep an eye on this door." Shepherd drained his glass and slammed it down on the desk. He shoved

Alfie out of the room, and slammed the door behind them both. Mickey heard the key turn in the lock, and the sound of retreating footsteps.

Immediately he began looking around for a way of escape. The office was windowless, and there were no tools to break out of the side of the building. There was no phone, so he couldn't call for help; no matches, so he couldn't start a fire.

Mickey looked desperately around the room. The place was obviously a drawing office, with a big flat table covered with designs for complicated parts of machinery. There were pencils in an old chipped mug, a T square, huge drawing pads. . . .

Mickey examined the door. It was loose and rattly, but discouragingly solid, and there was a big old-fashioned lock, the kind that takes a heavy key. Mickey had made rather a study of escape methods and a thought was stirring in the back of his mind. Something about a pencil, he thought. That was it. A way to get out of a locked room with a pencil and a sheet of newspaper. There were no newspapers in the little cubicle—but a sheet from one of the big drawing pads might serve just as well.

Mickey picked a long wooden pencil from the mug, tore off a sheet of stiff white paper from one of the giant pads, and went over to the door. Luckily there was a decent-sized gap between the bottom of the door and the ground.

He slid the sheet of paper under the door, leaving just a few inches so he could pull it back. Then he stuck the pencil in the lock, jiggling it in an effort to push the key through to the other side. It was a surprisingly long and

fiddly job, and Mickey snapped one pencil and had to go
and get another one. But he managed it at last and the
key dropped out onto the other side of the door. Gently
Mickey drew the sheet of paper back—and the key came
with it!

Mickey snatched it up. Pausing only to pocket Shepherd's whiskey glass, he unlocked the door, and found
himself facing Alfie. "Proper little Houdini, aren't you?
Now, gimme that key and get back inside. What are you
trying to do, get me in trouble?"

"You're in trouble already," said Mickey urgently.
"I'm offering you a chance to get out of it."

"I'm in trouble, am I? How do you make that out?"

"Because you're working for Shepherd, and Shepherd
is mixed up in something very nasty. I don't think you
know anything about it, and if you've got any sense, you
won't want to. But if Shepherd keeps me here and you
help him, you're an accomplice in kidnapping, maybe
even murder."

Alfie looked at him uneasily. "Pitching it a bit strong,
aren't you?"

"Do you want to take the chance?"

"I can't just let you go."

"You don't have to do anything. Go back over there
and play with your spaceship, and keep your back
turned. Let Shepherd work out what happened when he
gets back; you don't know anything about anything.
He'll probably be mad at you, but better him mad than
the cops."

Without giving Alfie time to argue, Mickey relocked
the door, leaving the key in the lock.

Alfie chuckled. "He'll think you really are Houdini!

All right, sonny, I admire your nerve. You hoppit."

Mickey turned and sprinted out of the workshop, across the yard, and up the alley. He didn't stop running till he was back at the tube station.

This time he sat quietly in his seat as the train rattled him back toward home. He was pretty sure he'd discovered something at Shepherd Electronics—but what?

Mickey leaned back with a sigh of content. He'd found the clues. It was up to Dan to make sense of them.

At that particular moment, Dan Robinson was trying to make sense of a crime that had happened—if it had happened at all—over a hundred years ago. With no clues and no witnesses, it wasn't easy. All he had to go on was the Reverend Catchpole's rather turgid volume *A Study in Evil.*

Catchpole wrote about the wicked Sir Jasper with a kind of fascinated horror, frequently interrupting his narrative with little sermons about the evils of drinking and gambling by the aristocracy in general, and by Sir Jasper Ryde in particular.

Dan lay back on his bed and ran over the basic facts in his mind. Sir Jasper and his boozing and gambling crony, the Comte de Berger, had both finished up stone broke, having sold their once-valuable estates and property and gambled away the proceeds. So the two friends had made a strange pact. They would play one last game, against each other, playing on till one was utterly penniless, and the other held the combined remnants of their two fortunes. The loser would then commit suicide, while the winner took the remaining cash and staggered off for a last fling at the gaming tables. If he won, at least one of the two friends would be prosperous again. If he lost, he would commit suicide too, and the two friends would meet, as they blasphemously said, in hell, where they would stake their souls in a game against the devil.

It was a pretty crazy story, but since Sir Jasper and his friend had been three-bottle-a-day men for years, they were probably blind drunk, which made it a bit more understandable.

Anyway, the final game had taken place in Sir Jasper's empty house, the mysterious fire had broken out, the count had died from his injuries, and Sir Jasper had never been seen again. There seemed no way of telling who'd won that final game—not that there'd have been much to win, by the sound of it, since both gamblers were down to their last few quid. As the Reverend Catchpole put it, "So died the representatives of not one but two noble houses, in a squalid contest for a pitiful handful of coins, all that remained of their once-prosperous estates. The Comte de Berger's impoverished descendants vanished from history. Sir Jasper's line was more fortunate. His baby son survived him, and with the help of his mother's family, restored the family fortunes through honest industry and built a second Old Park House on the ruins of the first.

Tossing the book aside, Dan lay back on his bed. Motive, that was the problem. It ought to be buried treasure—but how could it be when both of those in the story were broke? He thought of the Reverend Catchpole's phrase, "a pitiful handful of coins." He tried to imagine the scene, the two desperate gamblers playing by candlelight, with death for the loser, and for the winner—

Suddenly Dan sat bolt upright. "Of course—that's it! That's got to be it!" He grabbed a copy of *The Times* from his bedside table and leafed through it until he found the item he was looking for, then threw it aside. He had the why now, he was sure of it. All he needed was the who and the how.

He thought of Liz, Mickey, and Jeff. Maybe his Irregulars would come up with the answers. He had his theory now. All he needed was some facts.

One thing at least he could check up on himself.

He grabbed the phone book, looked up the Occult Research Society, and dialed the number. "I'm sorry to bother you," he said, when the secretary was on the line. "I just want to ask one simple question, about a Mr. Pearce. . . ."

13
The Accident

When Liz shot off after Mr. Pearce's car, and Mickey set off for the Underground station, Jeff was left at Old Park House alone. He didn't have to go anywhere. Mr. Chipsted was already in the basement, supervising his men. Apparently they were digging out the old masonry with a view to finding the extent of the dry rot and deciding how to deal with it.

Leaving Sir Jasper alone in the office, surrounded by piles of bills, Jeff went down to take a look at them.

The basement of Old Park House consisted of a series of interlinked cellars, all dark and gloomy and filled with piles of rubble. Mr. Chipsted's men were at work in one of the big corner cellars. They'd installed working lights, cleared away the rubble, and were now drilling away at the stone floor with pneumatic drills. An electric generator throbbed away in one corner, and what with this and the drill, the noise was shattering.

There were three men in Mr. Chipsted's gang. One was huge and hairy with tattoos on his muscular arms. He was using the drill. A tall gangling man with a drooping mustache was helping him, swinging a pick, and a smaller man, white-faced and black-haired, was clearing away the rubble in a barrow, tipping it into a pile in the corner. Mr. Chipsted stood watching them intently, some kind of chart in his hand.

Everything stopped when Jeff appeared at the top of the cellar steps. The hairy man switched off his drill and stood leaning on it, the tall man lowered his pick, and the little one halted his barrow. Mr. Chipsted shoved the plan in his pocket and swung around. "Yes, what is it?"

"Oh, nothing. Just came to see how you're getting on."

"If we had fewer people seeing how we were getting on, sure we'd get on a heck of a lot quicker, sir," said the mustached man in a thick Irish brogue.

The hairy man leaned the drill against the wall, spitting on his hands. "Aye, we would and a'." His Scots accent was as strong as the other's Irish.

The little man with the barrow said plaintively, "Old Sir Jasper's always hanging about like Marley's ghost, peering down yer neck. For all we know, the first Sir Jasper's watching us as well."

The hairy man shuddered. "Dinna be talking about ghosts, Harry boy. This place gives me the cauld shivers as it is."

They all stared reproachfully at Jeff. An Englishman, an Irishman, and a Scotsman, thought Jeff, just like in the jokes. He looked at Chipsted. "They're all a bit sensitive, aren't they?"

Chipsted gave him a gloomy look. "Can't blame them, can you, with all that's been going on here? They're a superstitious lot at the best of times, and with all this talk about ghosts and hauntings . . ."

"I see what you mean. According to that chap Pearce, there's actually a body down here somewhere. Maybe you'll find it."

The little man said, "If I find one single skeleton, I'll be out of this cellar so fast you won't see me behind for dust."

Chipsted gave Jeff a reproachful look. "Do you mind, sonny, we've got a lot to do. I'm having a hard job keeping 'em down here. Talking about skeletons won't help."

"All right, all right, I'll get out of your way." Jeff headed for the steps and then paused. "What are you doing down here anyway? Looks more like you're tearing the place down than repairing it."

Mr. Chipsted picked up a chunk of something on the floor and crumbled it in his fingers. "See that? Dry rot. Can't even start the repair work till we get all that out." He tossed it aside. "Now then, if you don't mind. They'll be clamorin' for their tea break in a minute as it is!"

Jeff went up the cellar steps, across the main entrance hall, and back to Sir Jasper in his study. The housekeeper was just delivering a tray of tea and cookies. Sir Jasper looked up. "Just in time, Jeff. Is there an extra cup for my young friend? Excellent!"

The housekeeper went out and Sir Jasper installed Jeff in an armchair, poured him tea and passed the cookies.

"How is the work progressing, Jeff? I really must pop down and see how they're getting on."

"Better not," advised Jeff, taking a cookie. "Proper bunch of prima donnas they are, won't work if anyone's watching."

"I suppose I really ought to leave them alone. But the work seems to go on so slowly, and I thought if I showed them I was taking a personal interest . . ."

"Where did you find Mr. Chipsted anyway?"

"I didn't really, he found me. I made a few inquiries when I was ready for the repair work to start, but the prices were so horrendous I didn't know what to do. Even with the money from the sale of the painting it looked as if there still wouldn't be enough. Then Mr. Chipsted came along to see me. He said he'd heard the job was going and offered to do the repairs at a very reasonable rate."

Jeff frowned. "Seems funny he should want to take it on. I mean, from what I gather, he's more of an odd-job builder. You know, attic conversions, knock two rooms into one, put you up a new garage. I reckon a job this size is a bit beyond him."

Sir Jasper sighed. "I'm beginning to think it's beyond me. All these mysterious events, Dan hurt . . . I don't know when I last had a good night's sleep. You know, Jeff, I'm very tempted to let the wretched place fall down in its own good time. That or sell it and move out. I mean, since even my own ancestor doesn't seem to want me here . . ."

"Don't give up, Sir Jasper. Maybe old Dan will sort it out for you. He's probably deducing away like mad at this very moment."

Jeff heard the sound of a car and glanced idly out of the window. A familiar black Ford was drawing up outside the house. "Well, now, friend Pearce is back."

Sir Jasper came to join him at the window, and they watched Mr. Pearce get out of the car and come into the house. "I wonder what he wants."

"I daresay he'll soon tell us," said Jeff. "I don't suppose he's come back to take the tour."

A few minutes later there was a rap on the door, and Mr. Pearce hurried in agitatedly. "Please forgive this intrusion, Sir Jasper, but I just had to come."

"You're very welcome," said Sir Jasper with his usual politeness. "Would you care for some tea?"

"No, no, thank you." Mr. Pearce sank into a chair. "I was on my way to another appointment when I suddenly had the most terrible premonition. A feeling of evil, gathering here, in this house. It was as if some terrible force was preparing to strike. Tell me, has anything happened?"

"Not as far as I know," said Sir Jasper worriedly. "The house is closed to visitors, of course, while the gallery window is being repaired. Mr. Chipsted and his men are still working in the cellar—Jeff's just been down to see them . . ."

A terrible scream came echoing from below. Jeff leaped to his feet and ran from the room, Sir Jasper and Mr. Pearce close behind him.

At the top of the cellar stairs they met the hairy Scotsman and the tall Irishman, carrying the body of the little Cockney between them. His arms and legs hung limply and his face was a mask of blood.

Mr. Chipsted was close behind them. "We must get him to a hospital at once. Carry him out to the van; it'll be quicker than waiting for an ambulance!"

The limp body was carried out to Mr. Chipsted's van and settled carefully in the back. The Scotsman climbed in beside him, and Chipsted jumped behind the wheel and drove away.

Sir Jasper was white-faced with shock. "What happened? For heaven's sake, what happened?"

"I saw it," said the tall Irishman thickly. "You'll not believe me—I saw it meself and I don't believe it."

"What happened?" demanded Jeff.

"There was a kind of rushing noise . . . a feeling of cold, of terrible evil. . . . Then a great chunk of concrete rose up in the air by itself and smashed poor Harry in the chest." He glared angrily at Sir Jasper. "You'll not get me working in this house anymore. There's evil here, and I'll not meddle with it. A million pounds wouldn't get me back down that cellar." With that he turned and positively ran off down the drive.

Mr. Pearce said sadly, "I fear I came too late. I warned you, Sir Jasper. I warned you time and again. I have some knowledge of first aid, and that poor man was gravely injured. There is evil in this house, Sir Jasper, and you are the focal point. I beg of you, leave this place at once, if not for your own sake, then for the sake of those around you."

Mr. Pearce walked slowly back to his car and drove away.

Stunned, Sir Jasper turned to Jeff. "He's right, of course. I should have listened to him before."

"Now just a minute, Sir Jasper—"

"Don't you realize that poor fellow may very well die . . . and his death will be on my conscience? Dan's already been hurt—do you think I'm going to risk harming you, or Mickey or Liz?"

"I know how you must feel. But at least talk to Dan before you do anything final. Anyway, perhaps that poor little chap wasn't too badly hurt after all."

Sir Jasper shook his head sadly. "I shall go and see

Dan tonight. But this time he won't dissuade me. My mind is made up. I shall leave this house tonight."

When Jeff reached the hospital he found Mickey and Liz waiting in reception.

"Dan's seeing the doctor," explained Liz. "We've got to wait till the examination's over."

Jeff looked at his two friends. "You both look pretty cocky. Solved the case, have you?"

"Naturally," said Mickey cheekily. "When Dan hears what I've got to tell him, it'll all be over."

"Don't listen to him," said Liz. "I'm the one who's really discovered something. What about you, Jeff?"

"Don't ask! What have you two found out?"

"Mickey won't tell me anything," explained Liz, "so I'm not telling him anything either."

Jeff nodded gloomily. "We might as well wait until we see Dan anyway." So they all three sat and waited, Jeff scowling and Liz and Mickey grinning at each other, until a nurse came and said they could go in.

To their surprise, they found Dan up and dressed, the bandage on his head replaced by a strip of plaster. He looked very much his old self again, was in excellent spirits, and had only the slightest trace of a limp.

"I've been discharged," he said cheerfully. "Apparently my ankle's sprained, not fractured, and the great brain has sustained no permanent harm. So come on, what have you got for me? This is your last chance to shine on your own before I take over and solve the case."

Jeff said grumpily, "I suppose you've worked it all out

lying here, and we've been rushing about for nothing."

"Well, more or less," said Dan cheerfully. "Still, no doubt you can add one or two finishing touches. Fire away!"

They let Mickey go first, largely because there was no way of stopping him, and he told of his visit to Shepherd's workshop and his subsequent escape. Dan listened in silence until he had finished, then said, "Well done, Mickey, that's the *how* solved. Your turn, Liz."

Liz recounted her pursuit of Mr. Pearce, and her conversation with his landlady. "So Pearce is a magician, not a medium," she concluded. "His landlady knew him up in Blackpool, then he turned up here asking her for a room for a few weeks. He's been coming and going mysteriously ever since."

"Maybe Pearce is a magician and a medium," said Dan blandly. "No law against having two jobs, is there? How about you, Jeff?"

"Are you ready for the bad news? Whatever you've decided, it's too late. Sir Jasper's had enough. He's going to leave the house for good." Jeff told them about the strange accident in the cellar.

When he'd finished, Dan said, "And that's the most suspicious story of all!" He looked around the circle of his friends. "Well done, all of you. We now know the *who* and the *how*—and thanks to my brilliant research, we know the *why*!"

"It's Shepherd, isn't it?" demanded Mickey. "I mean, that's not a burglar-alarm firm at all. And talk about a guilty conscience! You should have seen him go on at me."

"Come off it," said Liz, "it's *got* to be Pearce. I mean, a magician masquerading as a medium! How suspicious can you get?"

"So I suppose that leaves me Chipsted for my candidate," said Jeff. "Come on, Dan, which of them is it? Is it Chipsted?"

" 'Course not, it's Shepherd," yelled Mickey.

"Pearce," said Liz firmly.

Dan chose his words carefully. "You're all wrong, in a way. It isn't any one of them."

There was an astonished silence, and Dan went on, "As a matter of fact, Liz, you gave me the first hint—when you said Conan Doyle wasn't the only detective-story writer worth reading."

Jeff looked at the pile of thrillers beside the bed, and at the one on top. A slow smile spread across his face. "I see. So that's it—of course."

Mickey was jigging up and down with impatience. "Come on, someone tell me. You know I don't read Agatha Thingummy."

"You must have seen it on television," began Jeff, "*Murder*—"

The door opened and Sir Jasper came into the room, his face grave.

After his usual polite greetings he said abruptly, "I had a call from Mr. Chipsted before I left. His workman's in a coma with severe internal injuries. It's very unlikely that he'll live."

14
The Treasure

Jeff, Liz, and Mickey were having tea and cookies in the hospital canteen. Dan had asked to speak to Sir Jasper alone, presumably thinking that he stood a better chance of convincing him without an audience.

"You reckon he'll manage it?" asked Liz.

" 'Course he will," said Mickey confidently. "Talk the hind leg off a donkey, old Dan."

Jeff shook his head. "Did you see Sir Jasper's face when he came in? He's going to take a lot of convincing —and we're a bit short on real evidence, remember."

"Still, once Dan explains . . ." said Liz.

Jeff stood up. "No use sitting there arguing. Let's go and find out; they've had long enough by now."

When they got back to Dan's room he was sprawled out in the armchair, listening to Sir Jasper, who was on the telephone.

Dan put a finger to his lips and indicated that they should listen.

Sir Jasper was saying, "I'm sorry, Mr. Chipsted, but my decision is final. I simply won't risk anyone else getting hurt. I'm afraid our business association is at an end. I have left Old Park House, and have no intention of ever returning." He paused. "The repair work will be abandoned. Tomorrow a firm of auctioneers will begin cataloging the contents prior to auction. Once the

108

contents have been sold, the house will be pulled down. I have received an excellent offer for the site from a firm of property developers." Sir Jasper paused again. "No, my decision is final. The auctioneer's men are moving in first thing tomorrow. If you will send me a final account, I will see that it is settled. I have finished with Old Park House forever!"

Sir Jasper slammed down the phone.

There was a breathless silence. "I take it Dan failed to convince you," said Liz faintly.

To her astonishment, Sir Jasper actually smiled. "On the contrary; he was most eloquent."

Liz turned to Dan. "What are you up to, Dan Robinson?"

Dan went over to the phone. "Listen to this next call and all will be revealed!"

Dan dialed the number of the local police station. "Detective Sergeant Day, please." When Day was on the line, Dan said, "Now, listen, Detective *Sergeant* Day." This was a cunning reminder that Day's recent promotion had been achieved with the Irregulars' help. "This is Dan Robinson. Now, do you owe me a favor or do you not? Right, just listen then . . ."

Dan began to talk, and as they listened in, delighted grins spread over the faces of all three Irregulars.

The woods outside Old Park House were no place to be on a dark and stormy winter's night, and all four Irregulars were shivering as they huddled in the back of Detective Sergeant Day's car. Day and Sir Jasper were sitting in the front seat.

A dark shape loomed up at the window and they all

jumped. It was a uniformed constable. Day wound down the window. "All in there, Constable?"

"That's right, Sarge. We kept watch and let 'em all go in like you ordered."

Day climbed out of the car. "Well, just make sure you don't let them out again. Come on, everyone."

They all got out of the car and walked up the drive. Sir Jasper led them around the side of the house, opened a side door—there was no ringing of alarm bells—and ushered them inside. They were in a corridor at the rear of the house. Sir Jasper put a finger to his lips, produced a small pocket flashlight, and led them toward the cellar steps. As they came closer, they could hear the steady *chink* of pick and shovel. Then a low urgent voice. "That's it—we're through! Careful, man!" More pick and shovel noises.

Sir Jasper crept down the cellar steps, Day close behind him, Dan and the rest of the Irregulars in the rear.

There was an eerie scene at the bottom of the steps. A group of figures were gathered around an oblong opening dug out of the cellar floor. It looked like a grave—and as one of the figures moved aside, they could see a stretched-out skeleton figure in old-fashioned clothing. It clutched something to its chest with long bony fingers.

"Evening, all!" said Detective Sergeant Day cheerfully, and everyone swung around. Day shone the beam of his big flashlight from face to face. "Evening, Mr. Pearce, Mr. Shepherd, Mr. Chipsted." He flashed the beam on the faces of the three workmen—the big

Scotsman, the tall Irishman and held it a moment longer on the little Cockney. "Evening, Harry. Sitting up and taking nourishment?"

Lights came on in the house above them, and there was a tramp of booted feet. The group stirred uneasily, and Day said briskly, "Don't even think about making a run for it. There's nowhere to go but up those steps, and I've got men all over the house and grounds. Now, if you'll all file upstairs nice and quietly . . . I am a police officer and I have reason to believe you can assist me with my inquiries."

The tall Irishman raised his pick threateningly, but Chipsted said dully, "Come on, lads, no sense making things worse." He led the way upstairs, and the three workmen dropped their tools and followed meekly after him.

Shepherd was next to go. He shot a bitter look at Mickey as he passed. "Perishing kid!"

Mr. Pearce made no move, staring down into the grave as if unable to tear himself away. Sir Jasper went over to join him. "Tell me, is that . . . him?"

Mr. Pearce answered him with his usual grave politeness. "Yes, Sir Jasper, that is the body of your great-grandfather—murdered by *my* great-grandfather, the Comte de Berger."

Day came forward and shone his light into the grave. The whitened skull grinned eerily up at them. "What's that he's holding?"

Dan knelt by the grave, leaned forward, and took the bag from the bony fingers. It was a drawstring leather bag and it was very heavy. "I think this must be 'the pitiful remnant of two once-great fortunes.' The stake in that last gambling game. Isn't that right, Mr. Pearce?"

"I take it you must be Dan Robinson?"

"That's right."

"A pleasure to meet you at last," said Mr. Pearce gravely. "Yes, you're quite right. The bag holds exactly one thousand pounds. Sir Jasper won, you see, and my ancestor killed him in a fit of rage. Filled with guilt and panic, overcome with remorse, too, I like to think, he buried the money with the body, then set fire to the house to conceal his crime. As he lay dying from injuries received in the fire, he dictated a deathbed confession. Naturally the family hushed the whole thing up. The confession was lost for generations until I unearthed it among some family papers. Tempted by years of poverty, I decided to try and profit by his crime."

"You went through all this performance to get your hands on a thousand quid?" said Day incredulously. "A thousand quid, split between six of you?"

Dan said, "I don't think you quite understand yet, Happy. There are a thousand *gold sovereigns* in this bag. At today's prices, that's about eighty thousand pounds."

"Gold!" said Dan. "That was the key to it all. I knew there was something in that place someone was after, but I couldn't think what it could be. Sir Jasper and the Count were both supposed to be stone-broke. Then I realized if the money was in gold sovereigns . . . Pearce knew all along, of course; he got the whole story from the Count's confession. He decided to scare Sir Jasper away so he could look for the gold."

The conspirators had all been taken off by now, and Day and the four Irregulars were all sitting around a blazing fire in Sir Jasper's study, tucking into sandwiches and cocoa.

Suddenly Mickey remembered something. "Back at the hospital you said we were all wrong. You said it wasn't them."

"I said it wasn't any *one* of them," corrected Dan. "Well, it wasn't, it was *all* of them together. Like in *Murder on the Orient Express*. You remember? Old Poirot finds that not one of the suspects could have committed the murder because they all alibied each other. Turns out they were all in it together." Dan took a swig of cocoa. "Well, this was the same thing, in a way, on a smaller scale. It looked as if no one could get in to fake the ghost without triggering the burglar alarm, or being spotted by the workmen, or caught by the trained psychic investigator. But if all of them were in on it, they could cover up for each other."

"I thought Pearce had been checked by the police and passed okay," said Liz.

Dan grinned. "The real Pearce is okay—but he happens to be six foot three with a beard. Our Pearce just borrowed his name."

"How did Shepherd work the alarm business?" demanded Jeff. "That was a pretty impressive demonstration he gave us."

"Don't forget Shepherd isn't actually a burglar-alarm specialist at all, he runs a special-effects workshop, making stuff for films. He probably built in a radio-controlled cutout. Then he and his friends could switch off the alarm from the outside whenever they liked."

"What about the ghost, though?" asked Liz. "How did they do that?"

"Holographic projection, like I told you. Shepherd again. He'd be able to design the equipment he needed. I was always pretty sure the ghost was faked. What stumped me was how were they moving the equipment in and out with Shepherd's alarm system protecting the place, and Chipsted and his men searching it and finding nothing. Then I thought if Chipsted was in it too, he and his men could lug stuff in and out as they liked."

"What about all that *Exorcist* stuff?" asked Mickey. "The broken window and that."

"Same technique. Shepherd made the equipment, Chipsted and his men installed it, and Pearce turned up in time to trigger it all off."

"How?"

"You remember that camera he wouldn't let you touch? Another radio control. Explosive charges on the pictures and the window. Pearce worked everyone up into a nice old panic and triggered the 'special effects' one by one."

"What about the statue that fell over?"

"Dead easy. Pearce just gave it a shove when no one was looking."

"I suppose Pearce faked the séance too?" said Jeff.

"Of course he did. Bit of table rapping's dead easy. You fasten a cookie tin to one leg under your trousers and squeeze it with your knees. Makes a rapping sound. You have to wear baggy trousers, of course, but Pearce always did."

"And my narrow shave with the flowerpot?" asked Sir Jasper. "And then the spear later on?"

"One of Chipsted's men went on the roof and shoved the flowerpot down. The spear was a bit more tricky. I reckon they had a radio-controlled spring-gun at the far end of the gallery."

Jeff thought he'd caught Dan out at last. "Then what happened to it? I shot along that gallery like a rocket and I didn't see it."

As always, Dan had an answer. "Ah, but you did see Mr. Pearce with his big black box. He just took the thing to bits and stowed it inside while you were ghost chasing." Dan looked around triumphantly. "I don't know if I've forgotten anything—oh yes, the accident. That was a simple lie—it didn't happen. A scream, a bit of fake blood, and they whisked him away before anyone got a good look." Dan turned to Sir Jasper. "They'd decided they couldn't scare you off by then, so they started trying to play on your conscience. If they could convince you someone else was badly hurt and it was all your fault . . ."

"They very nearly succeeded," said Sir Jasper solemnly. "The sight of that poor fellow almost made me pack up and go."

"What made you so sure that was a fake?" asked Day.

"It was all pretty clumsy really," said Dan. "I think they were getting a bit desperate. For a start it was all a bit pat—Pearce turns up with his premonition, and bingo, there's a terrible accident. And look at the weird way they all acted."

"How do you mean?" asked Jeff. "It looked pretty convincing to me."

"Oh, come on," said Dan. "Pearce is supposed to know about first aid, right? So what do you do with someone who might have internal injuries? You leave him where he is and call an ambulance. You do not sling him in the back of a van and go roaring off. And roaring off where? What hospital was he supposed to be in? The one I was in was the nearest, and he certainly wasn't there. I checked."

Sir Jasper gave a smile of relief. "We checked all the local hospitals, and of course no such accident had been reported. That persuaded me Dan's theories were correct."

Day poured himself more cocoa. "So you decided to lay a little trap, young Robinson?"

"That's right. I got Sir Jasper to tell Chipsted he was selling out and knocking the house down. He gave them the impression that from tomorrow on the place would be swarming with auctioneers and demolition men—so they only had tonight to find the gold!"

Day shook his head. "Of all the complicated setups! Why didn't they just sneak in and lift the stuff?"

"Because they didn't know exactly where it was. They only had the vaguest description of the grave's location, and a whole new house had been built on the foundations of the old one. They had to do a lot of complicated and difficult excavation in solid concrete, and that takes time. You can't go digging up someone's cellar night after night without being noticed.

"I can see why they brought in Chipsted," conceded Day. "But why didn't they just lift the stuff under cover of the building work?"

Dan looked a little embarrassed. "Because Sir Jasper never left the house while the work was in progress, and kept popping in to keep an eye on them. He was driving them mad; they *had* to scare him away."

"And of course they didn't reckon on you four getting involved."

"I think that's partly why they put on such a big show; they had to convince all of us. Even when Shepherd clunked me with a chamber pot to discourage me, the rest of you were still hanging around."

"How do you know it was Shepherd?" asked Jeff.

"He was hanging around working the ghost stuff, and I got a bit too close to him. So he shoved all that furniture on top of me and gave me a swipe to be sure. Day found a very nice thumbprint on the handle of the chamber pot. It checked with the print Mickey brought back on the whiskey glass." Dan yawned and stretched. "I don't know if I've forgotten any particular bit of spookery, but it was all Shepherd, Chipsted, and Pearce between them."

Day gazed into the fire. "You know it still seems a bit much. All this expensive trickery and fakery and conspiracy. Was it worth it?"

"What do you think?" asked Dan. "Eighty thousand pounds, in gold. *Gold,* Happy. Negotiable anywhere in the world. Eighty thousand that could become ninety or a hundred if the price goes on soaring—which it will. What did they lay out? A bit of time and a few hundred quid. I expect Shepherd had most of the stuff in his workshop anyway."

Day rose and stretched. "Come on, I'd better run you back to your long-suffering parents. It's going to be a funny old tale in court, all this. I haven't worked out all the charges yet."

"Need there be any charges?" asked Sir Jasper. "Those men were more misguided than truly wicked, and they did very little real harm."

"They did a fair old bit of damage to your property," Day pointed out. "Not to mention poor old Dan's nut. There'll have to be charges, but it's such a complicated business they'll probably get off light—*if* they plead guilty and save us all a bit of trouble." He looked apologetically at Sir Jasper. "I think I'd better take charge of the gold, if you don't mind. It may be treasure trove or something."

"Oh, no, it isn't," said Dan. "It's family money found on Sir Jasper's own property. The state won't get a look in."

Sir Jasper picked up the bag. "Take it and welcome, Sergeant. It will be safer in police custody anyway. And if the law does decide it's mine, I shall give it to charity. As far as I'm concerned it's bloodstained money, and I want no part of it. Except . . ." He put his hand into the bag, took out four gold sovereigns, and solemnly presented one to each of the Irregulars.

15
A Triumph for Mickey

It was Mickey's idea that really saved the day. It was some weeks later, and Christmas was getting close. The conspirators had all pleaded guilty and got off with fines and suspended sentences. Shepherd and Chipsted simply went back to their normal businesses, and Mr. Pearce vanished from sight, presumably going back to doing magic tricks for skeptical kids, which, as Dan said, was punishment enough.

Sir Jasper insisted on giving the gold to charity. Since Chipsted had done no real work on the house at all, Sir Jasper soon found himself faced once again with the enormous cost of restoring the place—which looked like swallowing up his remaining capital.

It was Mickey who found the answer, one afternoon when he was visiting Old Park House. "You're missing a chance here, Sir J. Haven't you heard of the Chambers of Horrors and the London Dungeon? A place like this with a horrible murder and a ghost . . . it's worth a bomb if you exploit it right."

Sir Jasper listened in horrified fascination as Mickey explained his plans.

A couple of months later, the Irregulars were guests of honor at the reopening of Old Park House to the public. The upstairs of the house was more or less the same.

However, the art gallery had a new attraction. Every fifteen minutes the lights dimmed, a ghostly carriage was heard, there were echoing footsteps, and the ghost of the first Sir Jasper materialized before his portrait. But the newly restored cellars were the real attraction. Fascinated visitors were filing past a series of lurid waxwork scenes depicting the last fateful game of cards, the murder, the killer fleeing from the flames, and finally the open grave, where the grinning skeleton lay clutching its bag of gold. A few plastic gold coins spilled out for artistic effect.

Dan, Liz, Jeff, and Mickey stood with Sir Jasper in the entrance hall, watching the long line winding its way past the ticket office, up to the gallery and then down to the cellars. Dan said, "Well, I've got to hand it to you, Mickey. You came up with a winner!"

Jeff said, "Trust a little horror like him to see the attractions of a bit of blood and thunder!"

"Don't listen to him," said Liz. "You're a born showman, Mickey."

"Indeed he is," said Sir Jasper. "And I'm most grateful. I think Old Park House will make a profit from now on."

Mickey looked proudly at the results of his idea, the long line of visitors, the steady tinkling of the cash registers. "That's all right, Sir J," he said grandly. "Time your wicked ancestor earned his keep. I reckon the old boy left you a treasure after all!"